OPERATION MEGALODON
MATTHEW DENNION

SEVERED PRESS
HOBART TASMANIA

OPERATION MEGALODON

Dedicated to my love of cryptids, as well as shark books and movies!

PROLOGUE
INDIAN OCEAN

Captain Sheila Boyle sat on the bridge of the Exxon Oil tanker *Maynard*. Her ship was exiting the Persian Gulf and preparing to cross the Indian Ocean. She had captained the *Maynard* from the Gulf, along the coast of Saudi Arabia, to the Gulf of Oman, and finally to this point. Captain Boyle was scared when her ship was close to the eastern coast of the Gulf of Oman. Now, as she faced the daunting task of entering the Indian Ocean, she was absolutely terrified.

She took a deep breath as she weighed the five times regular pay she was getting to make this run against her life and the lives of her crew. She took a step outside of the bridge and onto the deck of the ship where she inhaled the salty air.

Her first mate, Greg Clark, walked up next to her. He stood next to her for a moment as they both stared at the ocean. The two of them stood in silence for several minutes before Greg placed his hand on the captain's shoulder. "It's not too late, Captain. We can still turn around and head back to port. We can all catch a plane home safely and see our families again."

The captain shook her head. "We could do that. Then we could sit back and watch as the country and the rest of the world crumbles around us in part because we weren't able to bring this oil back to the U.S. We can watch as people on TV and in our own homes go hungry because there is not enough gas to run the trucks that transport food across the country. As people who rely on oil heat to keep them warm freeze in the cold from lack of supplies or prices that are more than they can afford. We can watch as people lose their jobs because they can't afford to drive to work."

She turned to her first mate. "We can also try to make it across the ocean, and get paid an insane amount of money if we live to see the U.S." She looked back at the waters of the Indian Ocean. "We could also be dragged to the bottom of the ocean by one of the giant sea monsters unleashed by a madman."

The two of them looked out over the ocean again in silence as they considered their current situation. Six months ago, the Thuggee cult leader known as Rol-Hama had captured the world's cryptids and used a scientist's growth formula to enlarge the monsters to a gigantic size. He then had them fitted with a primitive neural implant that allowed him to

1

influence them. Rol-Hama worked the captured monsters into a frenzy and then unleashed them on the world. Two-hundred-foot-tall versions of Sasquatch, the Loch Ness Monster, the Jersey Devil, the Moth Man, and countless other cryptids attacked cities across the world.

The U.S. government was able to fight back against the enlarged cryptids with gigantic cybernetically enhanced birds known as ROCs. Their name was an acronym for *Retaliation on Cryptids* and a nod to the monster birds of myth. There were initially four ROCs who were controlled through a neural link with U.S. Air Force pilots. The cybernetic birds were able to reach incredible speeds, in excess of Mach 5. Aside from their size, speed, and strength, the ROCs also possessed steel-coated diamond feathers they could fire from their bodies to slice through their opponents. The ROCs deadliest weapons, however, were canisters of liquid nitrogen embedded in their throats. When the ROCs accessed these canisters, they were able to spray a white mist from their beaks capable of freezing organic matter solid within seconds of contact.

The ROCs engaged in numerous battles with the giant cryptids. The cybernetic beasts slew all of the attacking monsters, but in the process, two of the mighty birds fell. The final battle against Rol-Hama saw the remaining cyborgs, ROC 2 and ROC 4, battling the Lizard Man and the Mongolian Death Worm while a final assault was made on Rol-Hama's stronghold. The ROCs defeated the Lizard Man and the Death Worm while former ROC 1 pilot, Tobias Crow, slew Rol-Hama.

Prior to his death, the Thuggee cult leader unleashed his final attack on humanity. Rol-Hama revealed to Crow that he and his followers had not only trapped the world's terrestrial cryptids, but its aquatic beasts as well. Legendary sea monsters that had been reported since man had first set sail over the oceans were now under the control of Rol-Hama. The madman had the sea beasts fitted with neural implants designed to increase their aggressive tendencies. He then gave them the order to destroy all ships that dared to cross the oceans.

With his last breath, Rol-Hama destroyed the machine he had used to send the command out to the sea monsters, assuring that no one could send out a command rescinding the order.

The first attack occurred days after the death of Rol-Hama when the U.S. destroyer *Nevada* was off the coast of Africa. The *Nevada* was rammed into and split in two by a large creature covered in white fur with an elephant-like trunk. From that point on, the attacks steadily increased in frequency until nearly every fourth ship to try and sail across the ocean was being destroyed by sea monsters. The result was that worldwide trade was brought to a grinding halt. Food, oil, medical supplies, and countless other goods humans depended on to live were no longer able to reach the areas where they were needed.

ROC 2 and ROC 4 were mobilized to try and counteract the threat, but their effectiveness against the sea monsters was extremely limited. During their war with the cryptids, the ROCs were able to fly to whatever city the monsters were attacking and engage them there. The attacks on the ships were sporadic and over quickly. More often than not, a ship would report an attack and be destroyed before the ROCs were even able to take to the sky.

The U.S. government tried to address this issue by only having certain shipping lanes open at designated times so that the ROCs could fly over the lanes as ships tried to cross the various oceans. This approach was proving nearly as futile as it was to have the ROCS trying to respond to a direct attack. First of all, even with the ROCs incredible speed, they could not appear somewhere instantaneously. If the ROCs were on one part of the Pacific Ocean, and an attack occurred on the other side of it, there was nothing they could do. Splitting up the ROCs to cover more water was not an option either. The pilots of the ROCs had learned that their ability to link with the ROCs' minds and influence their actions was not affected by their skills as pilots, as they had originally thought. Captain Sheena Green suffered from permanent brain damage while linked to her ROC. Tobias Crow was nearly killed while linked to his ROC. It was Captains Lindsay Munroe and David Bixby who figured out that it was their ability to build interpersonal relationships with others that helped them to mentally sync with the ROCs. This revelation helped them to understand that the ROCs worked much more effectively when fighting alongside another ROC than they did alone. It seemed the ROCs had the same need for companionship and belonging that the humans did.

Munroe and Bixby's personal relationship quickly blossomed from one of friends with benefits to a couple who were deeply in love. As their relationship grew, ROC 2 and ROC 4 had become nearly as inseparable as their pilots. The close personal connection between the two pilots and their ROCs allowed the four individuals to work as a flawless cohesive unit. They were all aware of how to best support each other in battle by simply knowing their teammates so well. This connection resulted in the ROCs being far more effective together than they were alone.

While the concept of working together benefited the ROCs when engaging in battle, it drastically hampered their ability to cover large areas such as the world's oceans.

On the occasions when an attack occurred while the ROCs were nearby, there was little the cybernetic birds could do about it. The *USS Marlton* was crossing the Indian Ocean when it was grabbed by a colossal hairy hand that reached up out of the sea while the ROCs were flying above it. The hand started pulling the ship onto its side when ROC 2 dove at it and fired several of her diamond-coated steel feathers into the arm. The submerged monster pulled its arm back underwater, swam directly under the ship, and then punched a hole into its hull. The ROCs could do little more than circle above the water and watch as the hairy hand reached up from below the depths and pulled all of the sailors who had been on the ship to their deaths.

Captain Boyle's mind returned to the present as she looked back at the ocean. "What's the current location of the ROCs?"

Clark pulled out a tablet from his pocket and quickly searched for the location of the ROCs. He sighed. "They are currently two hundred miles off the coast of Brazil, escorting a series of oil tankers. If we're attacked, there is no way they can reach us in time to be of any help."

Boyle shrugged. "It's not like they've been able to stop any of the attacks anyway." She shook her head. "I say that we give it a shot. The last stats I heard said that seven out of ten ships are successfully completing their voyages. We have a seventy percent chance of successfully reaching the U.S. and scoring a huge payday."

Clark sighed. "That also gives us a thirty percent chance of drowning or being eaten by some monster."

Boyle turned away from her first mate. "We are going for it. We all knew what we were getting ourselves into when we signed up for this job. The crew needs this payday and frankly, so do I. With the economy the way it is, jobs are hard to come by. It's better to risk the chance of dying quickly on this trip than it is to quit and watch our families die slowly in poverty. Set sail, Mr. Clark. We are crossing the Indian."

Clark nodded. "Understood, Captain. I'll make sure we have round-the-clock surveillance on the sonar, looking for any large objects coming toward us."

The captain nodded then she and her first mate both headed back to the bridge of the ship. They were ascending the stairs to the bridge when Boyle grabbed Clark by the arm. "Just in case we run into something, do we have that harpoon ready the CIA is giving to all of the ships?"

Clark pointed to the bridge. "The one that's diamond-coated and supposed to embed itself into the monsters so that the government can track them? It's on the other side of the bridge door. God forbid we should need it. A couple of ships managed to tag monsters already. The thing is, everyone on those ships died." The first mate sighed. "If we do need the harpoon, it's ready to go."

For the first thirty hours of its voyage, the *Maynard* made its way across the ocean unscathed. A few whales were sighted on the sonar, but they were quickly identified as not being large enough to be a kaiju.

It was nearly noon on the second day of the voyage when the ship's radar picked up something large coming toward them. The sonar operator immediately called over Clark and pointed at the reading on the screen. The man's voice was shaking with fear as he told the captain what they were looking at. "The reading is coming in at over two hundred and eighty feet long! It's moving ten knots faster than our top speed and it's heading straight for us! There is no way we can outrun it."

Clark nodded, checked the position of the ROCs, and then sprinted across the bridge to the captain. "Ma'am, we have what looks to be a kaiju heading straight for us. It's moving at speeds faster than we can attain."

Captain Boyle's eyes went wide as she processed the information her first mate had just relayed to her. She looked out over the horizon. "What's the current position of the ROCs?"

Clark shook his head. "They are currently resting in the U.S. Even if they were in the air, there's no way they could reach us before the monster does!"

Boyle could see the crewmen on the bridge starting to panic. She realized that if there was any hope of saving the lives of everyone under her command, she needed to stay calm and act quickly. She shouted out, "We are going to take evasive maneuvers!" She looked toward the helmsmen. "Take us to top speed and have us move in a zig-zagging pattern. If we can't outrun the thing, maybe we can confuse it long enough for help to come." She then turned to Clark. "Send out an SOS to any military ships in the area! Tell them we are being pursued by a kaiju and that we're in need of immediate assistance!"

Clark shook his head. "We are not reading any ships on radar and even if we were, it's unlikely they would come to help us!"

Captain Boyle pointed her finger at her first mate. "The least we can do is try to outrun this thing. The most we can do is call for help and follow the protocols of describing the monster as best we can and hitting it with a tracking harpoon if it gets close enough to us. Doing those things will help the military to continue to take data on which monster may have attacked us and how many of them are out there." Boyle took a deep breath. "I plan to do everything we can to try and survive! If you are willing to help me in this endeavor, then follow my orders! If you are going to question me, then get the hell off my bridge and find somewhere to pray, because other than what I have commanded, it's the only thing that might save us!"

Clark nodded and did his best to compose himself. "You're right." He then turned and began sprinting toward the radio when the ship came to a complete stop. The sudden stop sent all of the crewmen of the *Maynard* tumbling to the floor.

Captain Boyle looked up from the floor out of the main window to see a colossal hair-covered hand reaching out of the water. She looked over at Clark to see him yelling into the radio, "It's a giant hairy hand! I repeat, a giant hairy hand! Anyone who hears this, please relay this information to the military!"

Boyle thought that Clark was about to scream when she saw him bow his head and close his eyes. Boyle realized what he was doing and she quickly sprang out of her chair. She ran past the other members of her petrified crew and grabbed the government-issued harpoon. She looked back up to see the giant hand coming toward the bridge of the ship. Boyle stood up and used the butt of the harpoon gun to smash out the bridge window. She aimed the harpoon gun at the oncoming giant hand and fired at it. The captain looked to make sure that the harpoon was buried in the monster's flesh and then she closed her eyes and began reciting the *Our Father* prayer. Boyle had finished reciting the first line of the prayer when she was showered by the broken glass of the bridge window. She had just started reciting the second line of the prayer when she and everyone else on the bridge was suddenly crushed to death.

CHAPTER 1

The water didn't feel cold. She knew the water should have been cold but for some reason, it wasn't. She stopped swimming for a moment and floated still in the water. Her long raven-colored hair drifted in front of her face as she looked deeper into the abyss to see her lover swimming below her. She could see Tobias' chiseled body moving gracefully through the water. Tobias Crow bared a strikingly similar appearance to the legendary Jimi Hendrix. The main difference in appearance between the Rock and Roll Hall of Famer and the Air Force captain was that Crow had the body of a U.S. Marine.

It took Tracy Curry a moment of admiring Tobias before it registered in her mind that he was naked. She looked down at her own body and saw that she was naked as well. She couldn't remember taking her clothes off. As she searched her mind, she also realized that she couldn't remember getting into the water either or where the water was. Tracy's mind began to race as she desperately tried to recall how she came to be submerged in water. She began to panic when she realized that she could not recall how long it had been since she had last taken a breath of air. Tracy looked up and she frantically began swimming for the surface. Tracy didn't know how long she had been underwater, but she was sure it was far too long for her to have gone without air.

The young neurosurgeon was frantically swimming toward the surface. She was pushing her body as hard as she could. She could feel water sliding alongside of her body at an amazing speed. For a brief moment, she considered the speed at which she was moving and how there was no way that she should have been able to swim as fast as she was. The thought of the velocity at which she was moving through the water was pushed aside when she saw the light above her. She could see the sun shining on the surface of the water and she knew that she was close to reaching air and filling her lungs with precious oxygen.

Tracy gave a final burst of speed and exploded out the water, shooting high into the air. She twisted in the air and then she crashed back down onto the surface of the water. She took a quick look around to see nothing but water in every direction. The lack of land or a ship within sight only increased her fear of drowning. Tracy opened her mouth and she took a deep breath of air. To her surprise, the air felt empty as if there was nothing to it. The young woman took several more gasping breaths as her body convulsed. With each breath she took, she could feel herself suffocating. Tracy was panicking as she looked back at her body to see it changing from the form of a young woman into a long, sleek, gray body.

She looked down at her hands and she unleashed a silent scream as she saw her fingers fusing together and changing color. Her eyes went wide when she saw her reflection in the water. She could see her thin face growing and stretching. Tracy tried desperately to take another breath when she saw rows of triangular teeth protruding out of her mouth.

Tracy tried to scream again but she still was unable to successfully draw air into her body. Tracy's body was changing into something monstrous and she was suffocating in the middle of the ocean. Somehow, a message flashed in front of her eyes.

Tracy, your mind is synced with MEG 1. You need to direct MEG 1 back underwater! If you keep her on the surface, you will both suffocate!

Tracy's mind couldn't process what the words she inexplicably saw in front of her meant. She felt as if her lungs were about to burst when she suddenly saw reality shift around her. The world seemed to slant and then blur before fading away. Tracy blinked her eyes several times as she stared up at the lights of the research wing of the National Aquarium in Baltimore. She was sitting up in recliner-like chair with her friend Jillian Crean standing above her, holding a helmet and visor with numerous wires protruding from it. Tracy looked to her left to see Tobias sitting in a recliner as well with a helmet and visor still attached to his head. The Air Force captain was grimacing and moving from side to side.

Tracy was disoriented and confused. She shook her head and then looked back at Jillian. She could see the bioengineer's mouth moving but she couldn't hear her. Tracy realized that she was panting. She took several deep breaths in an attempt to calm herself down. With each breath, she gained more control over her body and mind.

When she looked back at Jillian, she was finally able to understand what her friend was saying. "Tracy, are you okay? Did you get the message I typed to you through the neurolink about getting back underwater?"

Tracy looked at her friend and nodded.

"You had another incident of cognitive dissonance when linked with MEG 1."

Tracy nodded. "I think, I'm okay. I am back in my own body, right?"

Jillian had a nervous look on her face. "Yes, but we need to get you synced back with MEG 1 right away. Without you connected to her, the only mind MEG 1 has is her own. She is darting into the Atlantic. Crow is chasing after with MEG 2, but MEG 1 is faster and stronger than MEG 2. Even if he catches her, he won't be able to do much more than slow her down a little. Before MEG 1 hurts someone or causes any damage, we need you to return her to Baltimore Harbor." She placed her hand on Tracy's shoulder. "Remember, Mackenzie and I can see everything MEG 1 sees through the cameras installed behind her eyes. We are right there with you. You are not alone. Focus on that if you feel yourself losing your grip again. Got it?"

Tracy nodded, grabbed the neurolink helmet from her friend, and jammed it back onto her head. She quickly laid back down as the world once more shifted around her. The room she was looking at changed into a swirling vortex. An instant later, she found herself looking at water as she moved through it at a tremendous speed. Bright flashes of electricity were darting across her field of vision.

Tracy could feel MEG 1's mind racing with fear. Fear that Tracy had put there by first forcing the colossal shark to the surface and then trying to make it breathe air. The shark's mind was sent further into frenzy when Tracy suddenly broke her neurolink with the beast. Tracy tried to focus her mind, and at the same time MEG 1's mind, so that she could retake control of the beast. She let her mind run through the monster shark's two-hundred-sixty-foot-long body. Tracy was a scientist, and she did her best to think about the cybernetic shark in a scientific manner. As she was re-entering MEG 1's mind, she thought about the shark's creation.

MEG 1 was the aquatic extension of the Retaliation on Cryptids or ROC project. The ROCs were the giant cybernetic birds that synced with humans through a neural link that Tracy had helped to create. The ROCs had battled and defeated the cryptids that Rol-Hama had turned into giants with the Branson formula. When the ROCs defeated the giant cryptids and Rol-Hama was dying, he unleashed the sea monsters he had captured on the world. A quick response to the threat was needed. While the ROCs were giant cybernetic birds created over a series of steps from the DNA of prehistoric birds, the two MEGs were great white sharks, treated with the Branson formula, and given a few additional cybernetic upgrades. With the addition of an aquatic division, Operation ROC became the Monster Extermination Group or MEG. Given that the massive sharks conjured up thoughts of the megalodons of prehistory, and that the acronym already fit, the giant sharks were called MEGs.

The list of candidates to sync with the MEGs was short. Tobias Crow was one of the pilots who had synced with ROC 1 during the war with Rol-Hama. Crow's ROC died in battle with a Sasquatch the size of the building. With his ROC dead, Crow was immediately moved over to Operation MEG. Tracy herself was chosen next, due to her familiarity with the neurolink as its creator. She had none of the military training or background that Crow did, but her knowledge of how the neurolink worked made her the next best available candidate.

Reviewing the creation of the MEGs helped Tracy to focus on why she was sharing the mind of a giant monster shark. The next step in the process she used to regain mental control of MEG 1 was to extend her mind to feel every aspect of the shark's body. She let herself feel the shark's massive size and car-sized teeth. Tracy then opened herself up to the unnatural cybernetic enhancements that were a part of MEG 1. All of the leviathan's fins and her tail were covered in diamond-coated steel. These enhancements allowed the shark to cut through almost anything it brushed up against. Tracy acknowledged these appendages as an extension of herself and then she moved on to the most pressing enhancement made to the creature.

Tracy focused on the bolts of electricity darting across her vision and the entirety of MEG 1's body. One of the extra enhancements made to the MEGs was adding the DNA of an electric eel to the Branson formula. The electric eel DNA gave the MEGs the offensive capability of electrifying their bodies. Any monster that grabbed a hold of the MEGs could be hit with millions of volts of electricity should the need arise. The main issue of the MEGs using this ability was that it could only successfully be utilized in short bursts. If the MEGs gave off an electrical charge for a sustained period of time, it drained them physically, nearly to the point of exhaustion. Tracy knew that if MEG 1 kept swimming at top speed and giving off a continuous electric charge, the beast would pass out. It would lose consciousness, stop swimming, and ironically cause itself to meet the same fate of suffocation that it was fleeing from.

With her mind now fully aware of MEG 1's history and body, Tracy began to calm the monster down. She started subtly by having the creature turn slightly so that it stopped swimming straight ahead. After a few minutes of subtly coaxing the giant shark to its left, Tracy had managed to turn MEG 1 around. When MEG 1 was fully turned around, she was able to see MEG 2 swimming toward her. Tracy thought about that for moment. She saw MEG 2, not Tobias. It was becoming an apparent pattern that when she saw MEG 2 as Tobias and MEG 1 as herself instead of giant cyber-sharks; it was an indicator that she was losing her connection with MEG 1. It was this loss of connection that led to the panicked state both she and MEG 1 were in mere moments ago.

Tracy's physical body shivered as she thought about the next step in the process of calming MEG 1 and regaining some form of control over the monster. Tracy knew she needed to stop MEG 1 from sending out the electric shocks which were currently emanating from her body. In order to accomplish this, Tracy would have to deepen her connection with the shark. The difficult part about reaching a deeper connection was that it was exhausting for Tracy to do so. During the war with Rol-Hama, Tracy and the ROC pilots had learned that it wasn't their ability as pilots, or their willpower, that allowed them to deepen their sync with the ROCs. It was their ability to form and access the feelings created by deep and meaningful personal relationships with other humans. This connection was true not only between ROC and human, but also between human and human, as well as ROC and ROC. As ROC 2 pilot Lindsay Munroe and ROC 4 pilot David Bixby fell in love with each other, not only did their ability to sync with the ROCs grow stronger, but their ability to create coordinated attacks with the monsters expanded exponentially. The act of Munroe and Bixby falling in love literally won the war and had temporarily saved the world.

When she became aware of the correlation between interpersonal relationships and the neurolink, Tracy immediately knew the implications of it.

The brain worked like a muscle group. If you used parts of your brain at a high frequency, you strengthened that part of your brain. It's the *use it or lose it* logic of a skill. People learn Algebra and Geometry in high school, but ask anyone ten years later who has not used that skill in their job and they only remember the basic premise of the concepts as opposed to the skills they had mastered years before.

This same premise was true with interpersonal relationships as well. It was this concept that most affected Tracy. She was a female genius in a field dominated by men. Her intelligence and her work in research and development had conditioned Tracy to view romantic relationships as a nuisance rather than a benefit. This issue was exacerbated by the fact that she was one of the few women in her field. She had decided early on in her career that she wanted to be admired by her male peers for her mind and skills rather than her body. As result of this decision, Tracy had mentally shut herself off from any feelings of attraction or companionship that she might have experienced.

This decision had led to the part of her brain that engaged in these feelings to atrophy. It was only during the war with the cryptids that she found herself attracted to the stoic, and singularly focused on his work, Tobias Crow. At the end of the war, Tracy and Tobias admitted their feelings toward each other. They had no sooner had their first marginally successful date when they were told they would be syncing with the MEGs. This order came with the realization that the fate of the world now rested largely on the success of two people with poor interpersonal skills fostering a strong and lasting relationship.

Tracy and Tobias were just getting to know each other. To them, moving forward with a romantic relationship was like two blind people leading each other across an unknown land. This was one of the reasons that Tracy kept slipping into seeing MEG 2 as Tobias. Tobias was a very physically attractive man. As with most relationships, it was this physical attraction that first drew Tracy to the Air Force pilot. It was the most biologically based and easiest to understand aspect of Tracy and Tobias', or anyone other couples', relationship. The fact that it was a shallow emotion is what led to Tracy latching onto it when syncing with MEG 1. It was that same shallow aspect of the emotion that caused Tracy to lose control of herself and MEG 1 when they were synced.

As Tracy continued to try and calm down MEG 1, she looked at MEG 2 and she tried to focus on the best aspects of her budding relationship with Tobias. The first thought that came to her mind was how incredible Tobias was in bed. Fully aware that it was this thought that had caused her to lose control the first time, she pushed the thought aside as another message flashed across her field of vision.

Try to think of the things that you most enjoy about spending time with Tobias. Aside from sex.

Tracy knew that Jillian was trying to help her out, but mentioning sex with Tobias was like someone telling you not to think about white elephants. Once you are told not to think about something, it's what your mind is going to focus on. Tracy shifted her thoughts to working out with Tobias. While seeing him flex his muscles was obviously attractive to her, she also felt a quiet connection to him while they worked out. Tracy and Tobias both approached physical fitness with the same focus and tenacity they approached their careers with. Working out served as a shared interest they could enjoy together. Their mutual drive to be as physically fit as possible was something emotional they could bond over. Working out was a way of communicating with each other without the use of the far more difficult method of talking.

The young woman focused on the times that she and Tobias had worked out together. With her mind focused on that shared experience with another human being, she began to calm down. As a slight sense of peace began to move through Tracy's mind like a stream of cool water, MEG 1 also started to calm down. The aquatic kaiju began to swim slower and the electric shocks that were shooting out of her body began to diminish in frequency.

When MEG 1 had reached MEG 2, Tracy had managed to regain some level of influence within the monster's mind. MEG 1 and MEG 2 swam through the ocean back toward the Chesapeake Bay. The sharks swam at a relatively slow pace so that they could recover from the stress they had recently endured. It took the two monster sharks roughly an hour to reach the bay from a distance that they would typically have covered in forty minutes. As they swam back into the harbor, two crews immediately went to work.

The first crew dumped orca pheromones outside of the harbor. Aside from attracting any nearby killer whales, the pheromones also gave off the odor of the only ocean-bound predator of the great whites that the MEGs had once been. While the MEGs were more than capable of destroying a pod of orcas in a confrontation, their natural instinct was to shy away from the scent.

The second crew activated a series of electrically charged buoys. Like the pheromones, the buoys couldn't stop the MEGs if they really wanted to escape the harbor, but they helped to dissuade them from doing so. Due to their electric abilities, the MEGs carried an innate negative charge. Since the buoys had the same negative charge as the MEGs, they served to repel the sharks when they approached them.

While these first two factors served to dissuade the MEGs from trying to leave the harbor, it was the actions of the third crew that caused the MEGs to stay in the bay. Once the MEGs were in Chesapeake Bay, a series of small cargo planes and helicopters took to the air. They flew over the bay, dumping tons of fish, beef, chicken, and pork into the water. The moment that the food hit the surface of the bay, the two MEGs began to swallow it whole. The helicopter crews watched in a blend of horror and awe as the cybernetic sharks breached the water and closed their massive jaws on the food. Inwardly, Tracy breathed a small sigh of relief. She knew that she had nearly suffocated MEG 1 and then pushed the shark to the point of exhaustion. She took some solace in the fact that the Branson formula the MEGs had been exposed to not only increased their size but also greatly enhanced their healing abilities. The MEGs didn't have the ability to heal from a fatal wound like a comic book character, but they could repair damage to their bodies in days that would take a typical shark weeks to recover from.

With the MEGs safely returned to their enclosure, Tracy and Tobias both disconnected from their neurolinks. When they were both sitting upright, Tobias looked over at Tracy. "Are you good now?"

Tracy smiled. "I don't know if good is the word I would use, but I am back in my own body at least."

The two lovers were staring at each other, each thinking of what to say next, when George Mackenzie, Director of the CIA, and commanding officer of the Monster Extermination Group, walked over to them. "You two need to shower and eat. Then it's couples counseling and debriefing."

Being accustomed to following orders as a career military man, Tobias nodded and replied. "Yes, sir."

Tracy shook her head in defiance. "Debriefing is fine, but I am not sitting through another therapy session with a marriage counselor! For God sakes, Tobias and I have only been dating for a few months! Give us a little space!"

Mackenzie walked directly up to Tracy and looked down at her. "While you two are trying to get your relationship together, the world is going to hell. Two more ships were taken down by sea monsters and the ROCs are helpless to do anything about it! Also, if you didn't notice, your inability to move your relationship along nearly killed MEG 1 twice today!" Mackenzie shrugged. "Look, I am sorry you are in this position. Really, I am. Still, the fact of the matter is that we need to get the MEGs into the field yesterday. We can't do that until you two learn to love each other, or at least to love and trust someone!" Mackenzie turned away. "So for the sake of the entire human race, you two have couples therapy today."

Tracy shook her head and she turned to Tobias who was climbing out of his recliner. She looked at the Air Force captain, hoping that her words had some effect on him and that he would say something to Mackenzie. To her dismay, Crow simply reached out and helped Tracy out of her recliner. He then held her hand as they walked toward the cafeteria. As they strolled hand in hand, Tracy fumed with anger and did her best to minimize her disappointment in Tobias Crow.

Tracy knew that Tobias was just as inexperienced being in a relationship as she was. She was deeply bothered by the fact that Mackenzie seemed to have a say in how their relationship progressed. She wanted the CIA director to back off, and she wanted Tobias to come to her support in this situation. Tracy couldn't understand why Tobias had not spoken up on her behalf. She had seen the man literally run into a firefight with a knife. She found it hard to believe that he was afraid of anything, and yet he seemed unable to stand up to Mackenzie. Tracy shifted her eyes over toward Tobias as she thought to herself, *Is it that he won't speak up against a superior officer? Is it that he simply doesn't know that I wanted him to say something? How can he not see how much the idea of other people forcing themselves into our personal life upsets me?* Tracy shifted her eyes away from Tobias as her thoughts drifted from the shortcomings of her lover to self-reflection. *Maybe the problem is not Tobias? Maybe it's me? It's not like I'm an expert at this or anything. Am I somehow not making it clear to Tobias that I want him to speak up?* Tracy shook her head. *Do I really even want things to progress with Tobias? I mean, are we really a couple? Did we just hook up and now are staying together because the fate of the world depends on us?* She again shifted her eyes toward Tobias. *Does he have the same thoughts that I do? He is a warrior who is used to doing whatever it takes to save the world. Is he just pressing ahead in this relationship because of his sense of duty to save the world?* Tracy's shoulders dropped as she continued her inner monologue. *How can I expect Tobias to know what I want if I don't even know what I want? How do we answer all of these questions with the human race depending on us and Mackenzie and his crew watching every move that we make?*

CHAPTER 2
ASTRONAUT ISLANDS, CALIFORNIA

Virgil Simmons cracked his neck as he waited on the dock with his fellow rig workers to be taken out to Grissom Island. Virgil rubbed his eyes and took a sip of his iced coffee to help wake himself up. He looked over at his friend Ted Samuels. Ted looked just as weary and exhausted as he did. Virgil smiled at his friend. "What is this, like our fourteenth day straight of working a twelve-hour shift?"

Ted shrugged. "I think it's twelve for me. Maybe you're up to fourteen."

Virgil nodded. "Yeah, it's definitely fourteen for me. Not that I am complaining, mind you. With the current shipping crisis from the sea monster attacks, people are out of work all over the place. So if they are going to offer us overtime and ask us to work until the oil well goes dry, I say work while opportunity is there."

Ted nodded. "Yeah, with all of the Mideast oil shut off, they are sucking whatever's left out of the old Wilmington Oil Field. I heard the well was something like ninety percent dry before we started hitting it so hard. How long do you figure it's going to last before it runs dry?"

Virgil shrugged as he saw the ferry approaching the dock. "I don't know. It's one of the few oil fields left that is close to shore. The sea monsters are attacking anything that tries to sail across the oceans, so homegrown oil like ours is suddenly at a premium. My guess is that we will continue to drill in the well until it's all dried up. If the well is already ninety percent gone, then there can't be much left. I don't know what kind of work we will have available to us when that happens. So until then, I figure it's best to work as much as we can and to make as much money as possible."

Ted nodded and then turned away from his friend as the ferry pulled up to the dock. The oil rig workers all grabbed their lunches and piled onto the ferry.

Once the ferry was full, the ship pulled away from the dock and started heading back toward the man-made islands that housed the massive oil rigs. As the ship was pulling away, two Coast Guard ships armed with heavy automatic guns pulled alongside the ferry.

Ted tapped Virgil on the shoulder. "Even with the monsters not coming that close to shore, it's comforting to know we still get an armed escort."

Virgil nodded. "Yes, Old Uncle Sam isn't taking any chances. Until they get this whole sea monster thing worked out, it's blue-collar people like us that everyone else is counting on to keep the country moving." Virgil pointed at the large guns at the front of the boat to the starboard side of the ferry. "I was in the Navy when I first got out of high school, so I know the type of gun that thing is using." Virgil directed his friend's attention to the large machine gun in front of the Coast Guard boat. "That bad boy is a .50 caliber machine gun. It will cut through the steel hull of a ship like a hunting knife through paper. I don't know much about monsters, but I can tell you this, if one of them even came close to us, that gun would change its mind quickly."

Ted nodded. "Good to know."

The ferry's horns sounded, indicating the quick ride to Island Grissom was almost over.

Virgil looked out at the island and he shook his head in wonder at the man-made island. For a structure that was created to drill for oil, the island was a work of art. In the center of the island was a massive waterfall. The waterfall itself was created to help remove the water that had seeped its way into the oil and dispel it cleanly back into the ocean. While the waterfall served a functional purpose, it was still an inspiring sight to behold. The large screen that had been erected around the island to deter people from swimming or boating out to it were high and covered with trees at the top of it. The screens were sufficient to deter most people from trying to make it to the island, but the greenery around the tops of the screens added to the grandeur of Island Grissom.

Virgil had worked all around North America on various oil platforms. Most of the platforms that he had worked on were cold, mechanical structures. Virgil had found that working on platforms like that had a depressing effect on him. Virgil felt that when all he looked at was cold hard steel, he became cold and hard himself. The waterfalls and trees that decorated Island Grissom somehow gave Virgil a sense of peace and satisfaction.

Virgil knew that the world was going to hell. Monsters were attacking every ship on the ocean, the economy was grinding to a halt, and people were either scared or depressed. He was fully aware that he only had a limited amount of time that he was going to be able to work on Island Grissom before it was drilled dry. Virgil decided that he was going to enjoy that time. Virgil was making good money and working on a site that inspired him. He knew that times were tough for people and that tough times might be ahead for him as well. Virgil thought that most people would worry about all of the things that were going wrong or could go wrong and let those concerns overwhelm them. Virgil, however, took the opposite approach. He felt that it was when things were bad that it was most important to appreciate the good things in your life.

Virgil looked over at Ted and he noticed that his friend was staring at the waterfall in the middle of the island as well.

Virgil nudged his friend. "That waterfall is an awe-inspiring site, isn't it?"

Ted nodded as he kept his eyes on the waterfall. "Yeah, but what's that thing poking out from the top of it?"

Virgil looked at the top of the man-made waterfall to see a strange horse-shaped head peering over the top of the waterfall. The horse head continued to slide over the waterfall, revealing a long neck with round humps protruding out of it. The creature lifted its head into the air, showing a long serpentine body with flippers sticking out of the side of its midsection. The monster opened its mouth to show rows of serrated teeth. Then it unleashed a long and gurgled roared.

Virgil shook his head in disbelief. "What in the hell is that? Some kind of giant snake?"

Ted shook his head. "I think that's the Cadborosaurus. I've heard people report seeing him in the water going back to Native American times. They call him Caddy for short." Ted placed his hand over his eyes. "The waterfall is three hundred feet tall. That monster must be at least two hundred and seventy feet long!"

The men on the ferry watched in awe as Caddy wrapped his powerful body around the artificial waterfall that dominated the skyline of Island Grissom. A collective gasp escaped from the passengers on the ferry when they saw Caddy constrict his body like an anaconda. There was a cracking sound that echoed across the sky as the monster tightened his grip. A few seconds after the cracking had faded into the distance, there was a loud crash as the waterfall crumbled beneath Caddy's power. The passengers on the ferry all gasped as they watched Caddy and the remains of the once-majestic waterfall tumble onto the island.

Virgil and Ted ran to the front of the ferry where they could better see what was happening with the monster. When they reached the front of the boat, the rest of the passengers on the ferry piled in behind them. Virgil saw Caddy lift his head and neck into the air and then bring it down with his jaws wide open onto the island. When Caddy lifted his head back into the sky, Virgil could see a mix of machines and men in the monster's mouth. Caddy chewed on his grisly mouthful of food, and Virgil watched in horror as a mixture of blood and motor oil leaked out from Caddy's jaws.

Caddy then dropped his head back to ground level and slithered through the surface of Island Grissom like a living lightning bolt. Virgil watched in horror as debris were thrown into the air and the mixed sounds of metal being crushed and people screaming rang out over the water.

Virgil looked at the bridge of the ferry and screamed, "Hurry up! We have to get to the island and get those people off there!"

Virgil could see the terror on the ferry captain's face as the man yelled into his radio. Virgil wasn't sure if the captain heard his plea to make it to the island. He started making his way to the bridge of the ferry when the sound of machine gun fire ripped across the sky. Virgil shifted turned to his right to see the two Coast Guard boats streaking toward Island Grissom with their machine guns firing at the attacking monster.

Ted was standing next Virgil, screaming, "Yeah! Cut that stinking monster to ribbons!"

Virgil looked toward the island and Caddy. Virgil watched as the barrage of bullets bounced harmlessly off Caddy's thick hide. The two Coast Guard boats moved as close to the island as they could without beaching themselves. The boats then started circling the island as they kept up their ineffectual barrage on the sea serpent. Virgil watched helplessly as Caddy slithered across the island, crushing everything beneath its massive weight. The monster had just crashed into a drilling station when he suddenly stopped moving. Caddy's jaws shot forward and Virgil saw them close on something. When the monster lifted his head in the air, Virgil nearly vomited at the sight of the sea beast chewing another mouthful of human beings to death.

Virgil was still staring at the monster when he felt the ferry shift beneath him. He could feel the boat moving to the left and he looked at Ted. "What the hell? Are we turning around? We need to reach the island and help rescue survivors!"

Virgil turned around and started pushing his way through the staring crowd toward the bridge of the ferry. After making his way through nearly two dozen people, Virgil reached the door to the bridge of the ferry. He started pounding on the door and looked into the widow at the top of it, yelling, "You have to turn around! The Coast Guard boats aren't going to be enough to get those people off the island! We have to help them!"

19

The captain ignored Virgil's pleadings, but one of the crewman ran over to the door and looked through the window into Virgil's eyes. Virgil could see the horror and sadness in the crewman's eyes as he responded, "The Coast Guard is telling us to head back to port. They don't think there's anything that can be done to help the people on the island."

Virgil slowly turned away from the door and looked back to the island to see Caddy devouring another mouthful of people. He couldn't believe that they were just going to leave anyone who was still on the island to the fate that had just befallen their co-workers.

Virgil returned to the deck of the ship and he stood next Ted as they and everyone else watched Caddy destroy what remained of Island Grissom within a matter of minutes.

Throughout Caddy's attack, the Coast Guard boats continued to circle the island and fire upon the monster. When the beast had decimated the last remaining structure on the former oil station, Caddy roared and slipped into the water.

Virgil moved around Ted to see where Caddy had gone when he entered the water. His question was answered when the monster's head exploded out of the water with one of the Coast Guard's boats in his mouth. Caddy lifted the boat high into the air, causing the men on the vessel to tumble into the bay. When the monster's neck was fully extended, he crushed the boat between his jaws.

The monster then looked at the floating forms of the Coast Guard crew in the water around him. Caddy roared and then he plunged his face down into the water on top of two of the Coast Guard members.

Virgil could see a third crew member doing his best to swim toward the other Coast Guard boat when Caddy's head resurfaced behind him. The monster's jaws reached out and closed around the crewman, swallowing him whole. The remaining Coast Guard boat charged the sea monster, firing at its eyes and head. In addition to the stream of machine gun fire streaking from the Coast Guard boat, Virgil also saw a large harpoon shoot out of the front of the boat and embed itself into the monster's head.

Virgil had thought that Caddy moved fast on the island, but his speed on land was nothing compared to how fast the monster could move through the water. Virgil saw water spray into the air alongside Caddy as the serpent moved toward the Coast Guard boat. As the boat and the monster charged each other, Virgil knew that there was only one possible end to the battle.

When Caddy reached the boat, he quickly shifted his head to the side and smashed the boat to pieces. The crewmen who were on the boat were sent flying through air and crashed back down into the water. Caddy roared and then dove beneath the waves.

The ferry had just finished turning around when Virgil saw the first terrified member of the second Coast Guard boat dragged beneath the water. The same scene repeated itself twice more as Caddy slew the last of the men who had attacked him.

Everyone on the boat watched in stunned silence as the monster picked off the Coast Guard members. When the last person was pulled beneath the waves, Ted turned to Virgil. "It's over. Thank God, it's over."

Virgil was still looking at the spot were the last crewman had died. He shook his head when he saw Caddy's face return to the surface of the water. Caddy snorted and then started charging the slow-moving ferry. Virgil didn't scream or tell Ted to turn around. He simply hugged his friend and kept him facing toward the shore so that he could not see the oncoming creature. Virgil spoke into Ted's ear, "It's over. It's over."

Virgil had no sooner finished his sentence than Caddy smashed into the ferry and killed everyone on board.

CHAPTER 3
THE STRAIT OF MAGELLAN

Captain Thomas Mesa was at the helm of the cargo ship *Opal* as the ship made its way around the Strait of Magellan. This was the farthest point the ship would move away from land on their journey to the west coast of South America. Thomas knew that traveling across the ocean was dangerous due to the various monster attacks that were being carried out across the planet. In any other circumstance, he would have declined the offer to make the trip from southern Argentina to Peru. In this instance though, the people of Peru had recently been hit with a deadly earthquake. The disaster had decimated their country and many of the roads leading into it. The people of Peru were in desperate need of food, clean water, and medical supplies. The President of Argentina had pledged to help their neighbors. Bringing supplies from southern Argentina to Peru by land was a difficult task due to natural obstacles such as jungles and mountains. The damage done to many of the roads in Peru by the earthquake made the possibility of supplies being driven into the country even more daunting. Some supplies were able to be flown into Peru, but the damage to many of the country's runways only allowed small planes to land with limited supplies. The people of Peru needed help quickly and the fastest way to reach them with a large shipment of supplies was by sailing it to them.

Thomas had been a devout Catholic all of his life. His religion was one of the key factors that defined who he was. When he was asked to captain the trip along the South American coast, he was fully aware of the dangers that such a mission presented. Despite that danger, he felt that this request was God calling out to him to help his fellow man. Thomas was not the type of person to turn down a request for help from people in need, nor would he ignore a calling from God himself. Thomas accepted the offer to captain the ship of medical supplies and then he turned to his church to find his crew.

When Thomas made the appeal that this task was a calling from God and revealed to the people of the church how much they would be paid for sailing on this voyage, he quickly had an entire crew. Once the ship was fully loaded with supplies, it set sail. During the first part of the journey, Thomas hugged the coastline of South America as closely as he could. As they neared the tip of the continent, Thomas kept his eyes on two things. The first thing he was constantly watching was the ship's sonar feed. Twice during his journey, migrating whales had nearly caused him to panic when he thought they were oncoming sea monsters. The other thing Thomas kept peeking over toward was the special harpoon gun that his government had given him on behalf of the Americans.

Thomas could still hear the government agent's words as the darkly dressed man handed him the gun. "As pressing as your mission is, it is even more important that if you encounter a monster, you hit it with this harpoon. These harpoons are the only thing that will allow the Americans to track down these horrors and kill them. If it comes down to you dying or you hitting a monster with this harpoon, you are to hit the monster. Should you survive a monster attack without tagging it, you will be charged with treason. Should you die and tag the monster, your family shall receive three times your full payment and you will be credited as a national hero."

Thomas shivered as the agent's words ran through his mind. His thoughts were brought back to the present when he heard the radar monitor indicate it had located something. Thomas bit his lip and held his breath as he waited for the sonar display to give him another reading. When the display once again indicated a large object approaching from the south and quickly closing in on the ship, Thomas called for his first mate to take the helm.

The well-built sailor sprinted over to the helm. "What is it, Captain? Do we have one of those monsters heading toward us?"

Thomas patted his mate on the back. "I am not sure, son. I am going to go out on deck to assess the situation. Keep an eye on me and follow my directions. If there is a threat to the ship heading toward us, we will do our best to keep the ship afloat and the crew alive." Thomas looked over toward the specialized harpoon gun. "We will also do whatever we can to help put an end to this threat once and for all."

The first mate nodded solemnly and then took control of the helm.

Thomas nodded his approval at the young man and then he grabbed the specialized harpoon and walked out to the port side of his ship. The captain lifted his binoculars to his face and looked out over the choppy waters of the strait. He scanned the horizon until he saw something surface more than a kilometer from his current position.

The shape exploded out of the sea, and streaked across the surface of the water toward the ship. Thomas squinted his eyes as he tried to gain a better understanding of what he was looking at. Thomas could make out what looked like dark green scales covering a crescent-shaped head.

Whatever the monster was, it was swimming toward the broad side of the ship. Thomas guessed that he had roughly two minutes before the quickly approaching creature slammed into his ship and cut it in half.

He yelled to his first mate. "Turn hard to stern!"

On the deck of the ship, the first mate furiously spun the steerage, causing the boat to shift toward its stern side. The large cargo crates that were resting on the deck slid to the stern side of the ship. Loose articles went overboard and fell into the water. Several unprepared sailors lost their footing as well and fell to the deck as the massive cargo ship shifted beneath their feet.

As the ship was turning beneath him, Thomas wrapped his arm around the railing of the ship. He held the railing as tight as possible to maintain his balance while he continued to stare at the oncoming threat. Thomas said a silent prayer that the ship would shift enough to avoid the brunt of the monster's attack. Thomas felt his feet slipping beneath him and he gripped the harpoon gun in his hand even tighter to avoid dropping it into the sea. In his other hand, he felt his binoculars slipping out of his grip and he simply let them drop into the ocean.

The brave captain steadied himself and glared once more at the approaching sea monster. Thomas shook his head when he saw what looked like scale-covered human arms reaching out of the water and then dropping back down. The effect was eerily similar to giant green human arms swimming in a freestyle fashion. The beast's hands had five clawed fingers on them with a thick membrane connecting each finger. When Thomas was a child, he had seen the classic Universal monster film, *The Creature From the Black Lagoon.* The sight of the Gillman's clawed hand had terrified him and had been burned into his mind for the rest of his life. Thomas had that same terrifying feeling as he looked at what appeared to be that same hand, only this time it was as big as a house, and it wasn't on a movie screen. Rather, it was coming out of the water and heading for him.

Thomas was mesmerized by the motion of the swimming monster when he saw something that caused his heart to skip a beat. The beast lifted its head out of the water to show a face that was some horrific cross between a human and a fish. The monster's crescent-like head had a thick brow ridge with bright yellow eyes beneath them. In the center of the eyes were dark black irises. The monster's face had the overall shape of a human's but with protruding cheeks that gave it the visage of a puffer fish. The monster's mouth was full of long fang-like teeth. Thomas had no doubt that the beast's jaws could rip a large whale to shreds with a single bite.

The monster was only few hundred feet from the ship when it lifted its upper body out of the water to reveal a scale-covered, human-like torso. Thomas could see two large, scaly breasts protruding from the creature's chest. Thomas gasped as he realized that he was looking at a creature that defied explanation.

Since the first time ancient sailors set out across the sea, they had reported seeing mermaids. These creatures were described as half-human/half-fish females that roamed the oceans of the world. Popular fiction had depicted the mermaids as beautiful beings with the torsos of attractive women and the tails of fish. This depiction was far different from the tales sailors told of the hybrid creatures.

Sailors who saw mermaids described horrific abominations. They talked about some offshoot of the human evolutionary tree that tried to make its way back into the ocean and slowly adapted to living in the cold and turbulent sea. The true mermaids were not maidens that entranced men with their beauty. They were horrors that dragged men beneath the waves where they ate them alive while drowning them.

The giant Mermaid had nearly reached the ship when Thomas aimed his harpoon at the deformed nightmare. He was about to fire when the monster dove beneath the waves. As the creature was diving, a huge fluke-like tail rose into the air above the water. For a brief moment, Thomas considered firing at the Mermaid's tail, but he thought better of it. Thomas only had one shot at harpooning the monster. He had to make sure that when he took his shot, he was going to hit the creature.

Even though it was underwater, Thomas could still see the massive Mermaid. The beast was swimming just below the surface of the ocean. Thomas screamed in terror when the Mermaid's head looked up through the water at him. Like a colossal dolphin, the Mermaid hurled her body out of the sea and at the still-turning ship. The ship had completed roughly half of its one-hundred-and-eighty-degree turn when the Mermaid crashed into the front half of it. The front of the ship was torn to shreds as the Mermaid raked it with her claws and teeth.

The impact of the creature's attack caused Thomas to tumble over the railing he had been holding onto. As the bold captain tumbled toward the sea, he saw nothing but a wall of green scales in front of him. Adrenaline shot through Thomas's body. The effect of the chemical coursing through his veins caused him to have the sensation that everything around him was happening in slow motion. Thomas saw the creature's body in front of him and he lifted his harpoon to his side and fired. He watched as the harpoon struck the side of the monster's body and disappeared within her scales.

Thomas smiled to himself and then his body slammed into the cold waters of the Strait of Magellan. Thomas's body was shocked by the sudden extreme cold that was assaulting it. The veteran sailor's instincts took over and he started swimming toward the surface. When he broke the surface of the water, he saw the Mermaid circling his ship and tearing it apart. He watched as men, cargo, and pieces of the ship fell into the freezing water. Thomas said a brief prayer for the earthquake victims who would not be receiving the supplies they so desperately needed. When Thomas saw the Mermaid slash her claw down on several sailors who were treading water, he said a prayer for their souls. He hoped the Good Lord would spare the brave men a prolonged and painful death.

Thomas was still praying when the Mermaid tore the back half of his ship to pieces. He opened his eyes to see the front half of his ship lift high into the air. For a brief moment, he watched as the front end of the ship bobbed up and down in the water next to the huge Mermaid. Thomas began to tear up when the front end of his ship began to slip beneath the waves with members of his crew still clinging to it, as if it were some kind of misshapen life raft.

He heard two kind of screams from the members of his crew. He heard the long, deep cry of defiance from the men who were being pulled beneath the waves on the remains of the quickly submerging ship. He also heard the loud shrieks of terror from the men who were being scooped up in the Mermaid's scaly hand and brought toward her fanged mouth.

Thomas continued to tread water and watch helplessly as the Mermaid devoured what was left of his crew. A shock of fear ran down his spine when the Mermaid turned her huge yellow eyes on him. When the Mermaid dove into the water and started swimming toward him, Thomas expelled all of the air from his lungs and he stopped treading water. As Thomas slipped beneath the cold water, he hoped that he would drown before the Mermaid reached him. Thomas was immersed in total darkness and his lungs had nearly burst when he felt the scaled claw of the Mermaid close around him.

CHAPTER 4

Tracy Curry sighed as she and Tobias Crow walked into the office of Dr. Rhonda Vaughn. Vaughn was the couples' counselor who Mackenzie had hired and stationed on the base. It had only been two hours since Tracy and Tobias had disconnected from the MEGs. Tracy had time for a quick shower. After Tracy's shower, she and Tobias went to the commissary where they shared a meal in silence before heading to their latest counseling session. Tracy had tried to strike up a conversation with Tobias while they were eating when Mackenzie came over and sat down with them. He gave the exhausted MEG pilots a brief synopsis of the points that would be covered in the upcoming briefing. The key points included her latest failure with MEG 1 and that a new attack had occurred close to shore on an oil rig off the California Coast. In addition to the loss of life, and the fact that the sea monsters' attacks had clearly moved away from ships crossing the ocean to small islands, the loss of the oil drilling station had dealt another crushing blow to the already dwindling supply of oil in the U.S.

Mackenzie pointed this out as another reason that Tracy and Tobias needed to improve their ability to sync with the MEGs so they could be activated as quickly as possible. Tracy shook her head in disbelief as she thought about the last thing Mackenzie had said before the end of their conversation. "In two days, the MEGs are going to be put into action. If we wait much longer than that to act, the world we are fighting to save won't resemble the one we know."

Tracy plopped down into the doctor's couch and Tobias gently sat down next to her. As usual, Tobias simply sat quietly and waited for either her or the doctor to speak.

Dr. Vaughn first turned her attention to Tobias. "Captain Crow, how did you feel during your latest training session with MEG 2?"

Tobias shrugged. "I am still getting used to the sensation of moving through the water rather than the air. I can feel MEG 2 gliding through the water, but because of the difference in density between liquids and gases, it takes a bit more focus to keep MEG 2 moving through the ocean than it did to keep ROC 1 flying through the sky."

Vaughn nodded. "That is all well and good, but how is the connection between you and MEG 2?"

Tracy could feel Tobias shift a little in the seat next to her. "I think the connection is strong. He is responding well to my input. I have been able to sync with him and complete the objectives presented to us."

Vaughn smiled. "Yes, but how are you connecting with MEG 2 on a personal level? When you worked with ROC 1, reports indicated that your personality dominated the cyborg. Do you feel you're in a partnership with MEG 2? Or are you dominating the beast as you did ROC 1?"

Crow shrugged. "I am doing my best to let MEG 2's feelings and personality have as much input into his movements during our missions as possible. I am trying to direct him without taking complete control over him." Tobias sighed. "It's hard, but I am really trying to be as complacent as possible when I am synced with MEG 2."

As Crow finished his thought, Dr. Vaughn briefly glanced over at Tracy. Vaughn nodded. "I see. Why don't we turn give Dr. Curry a chance to reflect on her latest training session with MEG 1?"

Tracy nodded. "My brain is really having trouble adjusting to the neural link with MEG 1. What has it been? Something like three times since we first started syncing with the MEGs that I have freaked out while piloting MEG 1 and sent her to the surface for air where she started suffocating?"

Tracy shook her head. "There must be something within my brain that is having difficulty balancing the process of breathing air to sustain my body, while also having input from the experience of MEG 1 breathing water through her gills." Tracy looked at the doctor. "I have been trying to study the brains of creatures that breathe both air and water, like the mudskipper, to see what structures in their brains allows them to switch from air to water. I have also been studying the way that amphibians' brains change as they progress through their life cycle from breathing in water to breathing air."

Tracy leaned forward. "I am confident that I can figure this out and get MEG 1 running at optimal capacity."

Dr. Vaughn leaned back in her chair. "Dr. Curry, I can see that you are exploring numerous methods of brain function to try and better sync your mind with that of MEG 2. My question to you would be, do you feel that approaching the issue in relation to your brain as opposed to your mind is the most effective method?"

Tracy's intellectual pride quickly flared up within her. She was a neurologist with multiple degrees in her field. She was sure that the interaction between the brain and the body was something that could be verified and improved upon through the study of the brain itself. This concept was an essential truth in the study of neuroscience and brain functions. It was also what she felt defined her as a real doctor of science and separated her from people like "*Doctor*" Vaughn who studied peoples' feelings. Tracy shrugged. "The brain is a physical structure that controls the functions of our body and that we use to process, analyze, and then utilize information. There is something there that I can find to strengthen that process. I just need to keep pressing. The *mind* is an abstract concept created by people to describe the working aspects of the brain that they don't understand."

Dr. Vaughn shook her head. 'Dr. Curry, you were one of the first people to realize it was the ability of Captains Munroe and Bixby to strengthen their interpersonal relationships with each other that increased their abilities to sync with the ROCs. Wasn't it this realization that greatly improved their performance with the monsters?"

Tracy clenched her fits before replying. "Yes, studies show that the more certain neurons are used within the brain the synapses that connect them strengthen. That explains why when Munroe and Bixby's relationship strengthened, so did their relationships with the monsters they were syncing with."

Dr. Vaughn smiled. "Yes, and those synapses were strengthened by the feelings they experienced by getting to know one another better and caring more deeply for each other." She placed her hand over Tracy's. "You were able to see the need in Bixby and Munroe to strengthen their relationship, by opening up to each other, by revealing themselves to each other. It was through this process they were able to not only gain a deeper understanding of each other, but also of themselves, and their ROCs. I have no doubt that the connections in synapses were strengthened by their increased usage. Let me try to put my thoughts on this matter into terms I feel you can relate too. Is it possible that the strengthening of those synaptic connections was caused by chemicals released in their brains from feelings of love, joy, and companionship?"

Tracy's face went flush as anger welled up inside of her. She stood up and started yelling. "What do you want me to do? Do you want to Tobias and me to fall deeply in love with one another just like that?" Tears began to fill her eyes as she turned and looked at Crow. "I am sorry, Tobias, but I have never really been in a real relationship before. You have no idea what it's like to be the smart girl. Guys are put off by me for numerous reason. Maybe because they think I will go farther in life then they will with my career. Maybe it's because I do think too much about the interactions within the brain rather than looking at how someone else feels. Maybe I just suck at relationships and because of that, now the entire world is falling apart!"

Tracy looked at Tobias who continued to just stare at her blankly. She couldn't believe that once again he just sat there with nothing to say to her after her latest emotional tirade. She threw her hands up into the air. "The hell with this!" Then she stormed out of Dr. Vaughn's office.

Tracy walked briskly down the hallway back toward her room. Part of her still wanted Tobias to follow her, and part of her wanted him stay away from her until she calmed down. The young doctor threw her head back in disgust as she thought to herself, *I can't even decide what I want Tobias to do. So how can I expect him to know what to do?* She shook her head. *If I can't navigate my own emotions, how am I supposed to enhance my relationship with Tobias? Let alone a freaking gigantic shark?*

Tracy had reached the door to her quarters and she let herself in. She sat down on her couch where she tried to control her breathing. After several deep breaths, she started to regain control of her emotions. She stood up and started stretching her legs when there was a heavy knock on her door. From how heavy the knock was, she knew that it was Tobias. Tracy yelled at the door, "If you think I am ready to talk right now, you're wrong!"

Tobias spoke softly through the door, "I know you're not ready to talk. I don't know if I am ready to talk either, but I figured you guessed that already from the doctor's office. We have an hour before the briefing. I am going for a run. I thought you might want to join me. We don't have to talk. We can just run."

Tracy felt her anger and frustration seep out of her body. A good run was exactly what she needed to clear her head. She quickly changed into her sweat clothes and then opened the door to find Tobias outside the door stretching. She silently began stretching next to him and few minutes later, the two of them were jogging around the outskirts of the base.

CHAPTER 5

George Mackenzie was waiting in the briefing room with Jillian Crean, several high-ranking members of the U.S. Navy, a few senators, and the president himself. Mackenzie looked at the time on his computer and for the third time, he apologized to the people gathered before him. "I apologize again. Captain Crow and Dr. Curry were fully aware that we were supposed to begin this briefing twenty minutes ago. Our security cameras last picked them up jogging along the perimeter of the base. I have sent an MP unit out to retrieve them and bring them here."

Two of the senators groaned, but the president remained calm. "It's okay, Director. I can only imagine the pressure those two are under. I'm sure they are just trying to work off a little stress and lost track of time."

The admiral sitting closest to the president threw his hands into the air. "With each passing second, we are losing more resources and moving closer to the end of civilization as we know it! With all due respect, Mr. President, I think there are more pressing concerns than how stressed out the two MEG pilots are."

Jillian Crean walked over to the admiral. "Actually, if we want the MEGs to stop the sea monster attacks, then the mental health of Captain Crow and Dr. Curry should be your utmost concern. We know the better the mental state of the pilot, the better they sync with the creature they are connected too. Individually, our MEGs are no match for the monsters we have identified so far. If we have any hope of ending this threat, we need the MEG pilots to be in as good a mental state as possible. This will create a strong sync between the pilots and the MEGs, deepening the connection between the MEGs' physical abilities and the pilots' intelligence."

The admiral was glaring at Jillian and he was about to reply when Tracy and Tobias ran into the briefing room. The two of them were panting and trying to catch their breath. Tracy had her hands on her knees as Tobias walked over to the president and saluted the Commander and Chief. The pilot spoke respectfully, "My apologies, Mr. President. I lost track of time and took Dr. Curry with me. Any disciplinary actions should be directed at me. I take full responsibility for our tardiness."

The president waved his hand in front of him. "There will be no need for that, son. You are a world-renowned hero after leading the fight against those giant monsters and taking out Rol-Hama. Heck, you saved the world. You should be out enjoying the rest of your life and here we are asking you to save the world again. The least we can do is give you a few extra minutes to go for a jog."

Tobias nodded and turned away from the president. As he turned to face her, Tracy could see an embarrassed look on Tobias' face. She could have face-palmed herself for not seeing it before. It was another affirmation of how terrible she was at being in a relationship. Tobias was dealing not only with their new relationship, with learning to sync with MEG 2, and with the threat of the end of civilization, but with something else that he was totally unprepared for. For the past several months, since the very inception of their relationship, Tobias had been dealing with worldwide fame. After he had killed Rol-Hama, Tobias' name and face had been all over the news and internet. While the Air Force captain was never obligated to give interviews or speeches, he awoke every day to see his face on TV. At first, it was because he was the ROC pilot who had defeated several giant monsters when he was synced with ROC 1. Then because he was the man who killed the nearly superhuman terrorist, Rol-Hama.

Tracy walked over next to Tobias and she held his hand. For the first time, she saw what he was truly struggling with. Tobias was a soldier, a pilot, a man who was accustomed to doing his job and then moving onto the next mission. He was a private man who, for the most part, kept to himself. He had no friends or family to speak of. Tobias Crow was a man who was fully dedicated to his career and duty.

With the world first reeling from the attacks of giant cryptids, and now facing the current crisis of having its oceans closed off, the media took to Tobias Crow as if he were some sort of messiah. There were constant news stories on how he was going to be a pivotal piece of the new strategy to destroy the sea monsters.

Tobias was a private man. The type of man who preferred to operate in the shadows. Tobias didn't ask for or want the admiration or gratitude of others. He simply wanted to serve his country out of a sense of obligation and honor. Now that he was faced with worldwide fame, he didn't know how to handle it, and it was crushing him. Tracy could see that for Tobias, having the president fawn over him was almost more than he could bear.

Just a short while ago, when Tracy needed him to speak up on her behalf, Tobias said nothing. He did, however, come to her and offer her the outlet she needed to calm down, prior to entering this meeting. He was trying to be a good boyfriend to her. He was doing the best that he could to be the man she needed him to be. Now it was her turn to be the woman that he needed.

Tobias was a man of actions and not of words. Tracy may not have been overly skilled at communicating on a personal level as part of an intimate relationship, but what she was good at was dealing with men in positions of power.

She looked over at the president. "Captain Crow is being too modest, sir. I am equally to blame for us being late. I am not as used to syncing with a monster as Captain Crow is and I needed a little extra time to clear my head before heading to this meeting." Tracy tilted her head and smiled. "Please accept my sincerest apologies."

When she saw the president sit up a little in his chair and smile, she knew that she had diverted the attention away from Tobias and onto her. Tracy had learned long ago that most men felt the need to pay attention to the cute girl who played the part of the damsel who was in over her head. She was fully aware that by showing the least bit of vulnerability, men she was talking to would feel an almost instinctual need to protect her. She looked around the room to see the scowls on all of the men's faces softening. Even Mackenzie was no longer staring daggers at her.

The president shook his head. "No apology is needed from you either, little lady. If you need a few more minutes before we begin, please feel free to take them."

Tracy smiled. "Thank you for the offer, Mr. President. I feel that I am ready to go."

Tracy and Tobias sat down at the large conference table in the middle of the room. Mackenzie stared at them for an extra minute as a sign of his displeasure and then he started his presentation.

"As you all know, the threat of sea monsters attacking ships on the open sea has escalated to the point that World Wide Trade has come to a nearly a complete halt. Economies are failing and vital support systems are falling apart because of the lack of vital materials, goods, and supplies reaching the people who need them. The perpetrators of these attacks are sea cryptids. Like the predominantly terrestrial cryptids that Rol-Hama grew to gargantuan size during his first attack, these monsters have been subjected to Dr. Branson's growth formula. They have also the same neural implants that Rol-Hama used on his first set of monsters to give them basic commands and greatly enhance their aggressive tendencies. The result of these modifications is that monsters who were previously much smaller and docile are now massive and highly aggressive. Specifically, they have been directed to attack ships trying to cross the world's oceans." Mackenzie changed the image on his presentation to show an example of the modified harpoon that was being distributed to ship captains. "Our response to this threat has been twofold. The first step was to equip as many merchant, naval, and Coast Guard ships as we could with these harpoon guns. The harpoons function as both tracking devices and as an information gathering and intelligence system. Every monster that we have tagged with these harpoons we can now identify and locate." Mackenzie took a deep breath. "Many of the creatures that I am about to show you will appear as they are not inherently aquatic. I assure you not only that they are aquatic but that they have also been reported by sailors for hundreds, if not thousands, of years."

The first creature that Mackenzie showed the group was the serpentine-like monster that had attacked Astronaut Island. "This monster is known as Cadborosaurus or Caddy for short. It has the overall appearance of what we would think of as a traditional sea serpent. It has a long snake-like body with large humps across its back, a horse-like face, and sharp dagger-like teeth. Witnesses have seen this creature in the San Francisco Bay area for several decades. Like all of the other monsters that we will review today, this normally peaceful creature was exposed to Rol-Hama's growth serum which caused the creature to grow to a size of two hundred and eighty feet long. The serum has also greatly exaggerated its aggressive tendencies. This monster has been patrolling the Pacific Ocean from South America to Alaska and as far out as Hawaii. The creature recently attacked an oil rig off the coast of California."

Mackenzie changed the screen to show what looked like a large pilot whale covered in bright white fur with a think elephantine trunk. Mackenzie saw the president's face contort at the sight of the strange creature. Mackenzie sighed. "As I said, we are dealing with very unusual creatures. This beast is popularly known as Trunko."

The president shook his head. "Trunko? Really?"

Mackenzie shrugged. "Just to be clear, Mr. President. These aquatic cryptids all had names long before we encountered them. We are not responsible for what people have dubbed them." Mackenzie redirected the conversation back to the monster in question. "As I was saying, this creature is called Trunko. He was first spotted off the coast of South Africa in 1924. Trunko was engaged in a battle with two killer whales and the encounter was witnessed by several hundred people who watched the battle from the shore. Both Trunko and the orcas seemingly died during the encounter and Trunko was reported to have washed ashore. The cryptid laid on the beach for several days before returning to the ocean. The original size of the monster is unverified, but he is now reportedly over three hundred feet long. The beast seems to be physically strong and durable as he has shattered several tankers to pieces by ramming into them. He is currently attacking ships in the Atlantic Ocean between the African and South American coasts."

The screen changed to the grotesque form of the giant mermaid who was patrolling the ocean around the Strait of Magellan. When Tracy saw the horrific creature with its unique blend of human and fish-like qualities, her body shook with disgust. She quietly reached over and grabbed Tobias' hand. The pilot gave her hand a squeeze and the sensation of feeling Tobias' strong grip helped to calm Tracy down a little.

Mackenzie gestured toward the screen. "This creature is what is commonly referred to as a Mermaid."

The president shook his head. "That thing looks more like something from a Lovecraft story than it does a Disney movie."

Mackenzie nodded. "Yes, it seems that the idea of Ariel is a far cry from what a mermaid truly is. The reason that manatees were mistaken for mermaids makes a lot more sense when you see this demon. No one would mistake a manatee for a beautiful woman but at a distance, they could mistake it for one of these things." Mackenzie changed the view to another shot of the Mermaid. "This monster is two hundred and twenty feet long. It's long arms and hands could give it a significant advantage over the MEGs in battle. The captain of the ship that was carrying supplies to earthquake victims managed to tag this monster with one of our harpoons. The readings we are getting from the harpoon indicate the mermaid is able to move at least as fast as the top speed we have so far clocked on the MEGs." Mackenzie shrugged. "It's entirely possible the Mermaid is both faster and more agile in the water than the MEGs." He shifted his eyes toward Tracy and Tobias. "When engaging this monster, the MEGs will need to have their coordinated attacks working at optimal efficiency."

The next creature in Mackenzie's presentation was the most recognizable and normal of all the monsters that he was covering. "This giant octopus which we are calling Otaka has been terrorizing the Pacific Ocean predominantly around Japan, although he has traveled as far as Australia. When his tentacles are fully spread out, this cephalopod is nearly five hundred feet wide. That would make the octopus about twice the size of the MEGs."

Tobias raised his hand. "Sir, is this a monster that already existed or is it simply an octopus that Rol-Hama's men treated with the Branson formula?"

Mackenzie shrugged. "The readings coming from the harpoon indicated that this beast has been exposed to the Branson formula. We are unsure if it was an existing giant that grew larger or if as you suggested was at one time a typical octopus."

Crow nodded. "If it was an already existing but unidentified monster, is there a possibility that it could have abilities not exhibited by a typical octopus?"

Mackenzie nodded. "The readings coming from the harpoon indicate that this creature has hooks embedded in his suckers. When engaging this monster, proceed with caution. If he is able to wrap the MEGs up in his tentacles, those hooks could do some serious damage to them."

Mackenzie looked around the room to see if there were any follow-up questions. When no else voiced any secondary concerns, he went to the next monster in his presentation. The image of a large hairy humanoid being moving around underwater filled the screen. Tracy was thinking that the monster looked like some kind of aquatic orangutan with a disturbingly human face when she felt Tobias' body shaking next her.

Tracy had only known Tobias for a few months, but in that time, she had never seen her lover be anything but completely fearless. As she looked at Tobias, she could see that the image on the screen was terrifying to him. At first, Tracy was unable to understand why Tobias was affected in such a way by the primate-like monster. She was thinking that perhaps Tobias was upset by the monster's all-too-human-looking face when she recalled Tobias' last battle with ROC 1.

ROC 1 had been dispatched to kill a giant Sasquatch that was wreaking havoc along the Western coast of the United States. Tobias and ROC 1 had already single-handedly slain several giant cryptids and it was assumed that they would be equally successful in this mission. That assumption was quickly proven wrong when ROC 1 engaged the Sasquatch. The cryptid's strength, speed, and durability were far greater than any of the monsters they had encountered until that point. The Sasquatch shrugged off ROC 1's attacks and grabbed a hold of the cybernetic bird. The Sasquatch was crushing ROC 1 to death while Tobias was still synced with him. Tobias experienced every sensation that ROC 1 was feeling as the Sasquatch tore it limb from limb. In order to save his own life, Tobias had to break his connection to ROC 1.

While Tobias managed to survive, he still felt what it was like to be as close to death as possible without actually dying. This time, it was Tracy who squeezed Tobias' hand in order to lend him some of her strength. He looked over at her and she held his gaze. She nodded silently at him, indicating that she was aware of his distress and that she would do whatever she could to help him deal with it.

Tobias nodded back to Tracy and then returned his gaze to the screen. As she felt her lover's body slowly stop trembling, Tracy hoped that they had just taken a small step toward deepening the extent of their suddenly all-important relationship.

The president was staring at the ape-like monster as he called out to Mackenzie, "That thing lives underwater? It looks like it belongs in a jungle or something!"

Mackenzie shook his head. "This is definitely the most perplexing of all of the cryptids we have encountered so far. As far as we can tell, this monster is the Shojo. It is sort of an underwater orangutan who stands at two hundred and seventy feet tall. The monster was generally considered to be a creature of Japanese folklore, but like giants in the Western World, there are reports of the monster being sighted in real life. Obviously, we can now confirm those reports are true. This monster has been attacking ships in the Indian Ocean."

The president shook his head. "Why would a creature that looks like it was developed for life on land live in the ocean?"

Mackenzie shrugged. "What little we know about the monster suggests that it may be evidence of what is known as the Aquatic Ape Theory. The gist of this theory is that a branch of early primates developed traits which made it more beneficial for them to live in the water than it did to stay on land. While this idea is seen as outlandish, there is some precedent for it. The ancestors of whales are known to have been land-dwelling creatures. The theory is that if whales could have evolved in such a way that they became better adapted for life in the ocean, the same could have happened to a species of primate as well."

This time, it was Tracy who raised her hand with a question. "Mackenzie, given this creature's anatomical features, is it possible that this monster could come ashore?"

Mackenzie shrugged. "We do not have any reports of the Shojo making landfall. The information that we have from the harpoon in the monster confirms that it has gills, but we can't say for sure if the monster has lungs or not. However, in order to be prepared for a potential land-based attack, we will reposition ROC 2 and ROC 4 to a site on the east coast of the African continent. Should the Shojo try to come ashore in Africa, Europe, or parts of Asia, the ROCs will be in a position to respond to the threat."

Mackenzie switched the screen to show a world map with a red line that started at Baltimore and then snaked its way around the world's oceans. There were numerous dots that blinked on the screen near the line. The CIA director pointed at the line. "This is the proposed path we are suggesting the MEGs take as they engage these monsters." Mackenzie zoomed the screen in on a dot that was in the middle of the Atlantic Ocean. "The MEGs will leave from Chesapeake Bay and make their way into the Atlantic. Trunko will be their first target. Our current readings have the monster right in the middle of the Atlantic Ocean between South America and Africa. If two orcas were able to defeat this thing when he was smaller, we are hoping the MEGs will be just as effective on the bigger version."

Mackenzie next zoomed in on the part of the red line that went around the tip of South America. "After dealing with Trunko in the Atlantic, the MEGs will enter the Strait of Magellan where they will engage the Mermaid. Again, this monster is able to move at incredible speeds, so be sure to coordinate the MEGs' attacks."

Mackenzie followed the red line up the coasts of South and Central America. He stopped at a blinking light off the coast of California. "Once the MEGs have entered the Pacific, their first target will be Caddy. Right now, the sea serpent is still swimming around off the coast of California."

Mackenzie continued along the red line as it made its way across the Pacific Ocean to Japan. "Otaka is slithering around on the bottom of the Pacific off the coast of Japan. The MEGs will engage him there. Sharks are natural predators of octopi, so when you reach this point, you may want to rely as much on the MEGs' natural instincts as you do your own." Mackenzie looked directly at Tracy and Tobias. "Your ability to utilize the MEGs' instincts successfully will of course depend on how well you are able to sync with them."

The CIA director then followed the line around the northern part of Australia and into the Indian Ocean. In the center of the Indian Ocean was the last blinking red dot. Mackenzie zoomed in on the dot. "The final monster we will attack is the Shojo."

Mackenzie looked around the room. "If there are no additional questions, I recommend that we put an immediate stop to all oceanic traffic as we prepare to unleash the MEGs."

The president stood up. "I will give the order immediately to all U.S. ships. Then I will contact our ambassadors around the world and have them convey the same suggestion to every nation that still has active ships on the ocean."

Mackenzie nodded then he looked at Tracy and Tobias. "You two will be given the coordinates for Trunko. You are to briefly sync with the MEGs and set them on a path to attack the first target. Once they are on their way, I want you to try and get some sleep. From this point on, that will be a luxury you will only be able to enjoy as the MEGs move from mission to mission."

Tobias replied with a prompt. "Yes, sir."

Tracy simply nodded and stood up. The two of them continued to hold hands as they left the debriefing room.

Once the two MEG pilots had left the room, the president walked over to Mackenzie. "What's the status of their relationship? Have they reached the point where they have developed enough of an ability to interact with another person to fully sync with the MEGs and make this mission a success?"

Mackenzie shook his head. "According to our therapist, they are nowhere near where they need to be in terms of understanding each other or the MEGs. They are both loners who are used to relying only on themselves." He turned to the president. "Honestly, I don't think they are ready for this mission. I also don't know if they will ever reach the level of being able to support a successful relationship with anyone, let alone each other. What I do know is that if we don't get international shipping up and running again soon, a lot of people are going to die and nations are going to collapse. Curry and Crow may not be the best people for this mission, but we don't have time to train anyone else to sync with a giant monster. We either send them out on this mission now and hope for the best, or we prepare to live in an entirely different and darker world than we are used too."

CHAPTER 6

After leaving the briefing room, Tracy and Tobias made their way back toward the neurolink recliners that connected them with MEGs. The two lovers sat down in their recliners and placed the neurolink helmets on their heads. Tracy was exhausted, but she tried to remain calm and focused as she rebonded with MEG 1's mind. As she was merging with the shark's mind, she could feel the beast's primal instincts flooding into her thoughts. Tracy took a deep breath, closed her eyes, and did her best to accept MEG 1's instincts without trying to embrace or reject them. Tracy compared navigating the influx of MEG 1's instincts to one of her favorite hobbies. Tracy was an avid surfer and she felt the best way to ride a powerful wave was to go with the wave's strength. If she tried to turn into the wave, it would collapse on her and toss her off her board. If she tried to turn away from the wave, she would lose it completely. The best method for riding the wave was to find the middle ground of not embracing the wave or rejecting it. The moment that Tracy found that middle ground with MEG 1's mind, she felt at peace.

She opened her eyes to see the water of the Chesapeake swirling around her. Through MEG 1's electroreception abilities, Tracy was able to detect nearly everything living in the bay by its electromagnetic field. She could sense everything from MEG 2 swimming behind her, to seagulls floating on the surface of the water, to tiny shrimp and crabs crawling on the floor of the bay itself. As Tracy let her thoughts merge with MEG 1, she began to better understand the beauty of being part of the supposed monster that she was synced with. During her first few times syncing with MEG 1, Tracy was fighting against the shark to keep her mind, what she thought of as her very self, from merging with the creature. With each sync since that point, Tracy had grown slightly more comfortable syncing with the enhanced beast. At her very core, she was a scientist and part of the process that was helping her to sync better with MEG 1 was the opportunity to study how a shark perceived reality. The more that Tracy opened her mind to MEG 1, the more information she was able to gather on how MEG 1 was able to use her amazing senses to navigate the world around her and react to stimuli.

When she felt a large presence moving up beside her, MEG 1 instinctively shifted her eyes to the left. Tracy was relieved when she saw MEG 2 and not Tobias swimming in the bay next to her. MEG 1 circled the harbor a few times as the crews at the entrance to the harbor dumped in pheromones that would cancel out the orca scent they had deposited there earlier. With the scent barrier gone, Tracy guided MEG 1 into the open ocean and MEG 2 followed her. The two cybernetic sharks started swimming down the Gulf Stream as Tracy focused on the first stop at the center of the Atlantic Ocean. Once Tracy was confident that MEG 1 would continue on the path she had laid out, she disconnected from the neurolink. She sat up to see Tobias disconnecting as well.

Jillian Crean was sitting at a nearby computer console. She looked up from her monitor. "The MEGs seem to be following your last direction. We will have a cargo plane dump food in front of them at the midpoint of their journey." Jillian smiled at Tracy. "You two look exhausted. Like we talked about earlier, you have twenty-four hours until the MEGs reach the first target. Why don't you get some sleep for the next few hours? Then take most of tomorrow for yourselves. I'll tell Mackenzie that we have some readings from the neurolink which shows undue stress and mental exhaustion on your part. I can buy you two at least a day of no briefings or counseling sessions."

Tracy smiled. "Thank you, Jillian." Tobias simply sat up and nodded silently. The weary couple walked next to each other as they made their way back to their quarters. As they walked, Tracy thought about how she had found the middle ground with MEG 1. She accepted the shark's instincts without letting them overwhelm her or outright rejecting them. She realized that taking the same approach with Tobias might be what she needed to do if she had any hope of having something lasting with the man. Tracy was inwardly chiding herself for not realizing a concept which should have been obvious to any normal person earlier.

Tracy opened the door to their quarters and entered it. Tobias followed her and closed the door. The moment that the door closed, Tobias wrapped his arm around Tracy and he pulled her closer to him. He then leaned in and kissed her passionately. Tracy kissed him back, but in her mind, she sighed. Tobias wanted to have sex and she was exhausted. Tracy was debating if it would be better for their relationship to acquiesce to Tobias' desires or to let him down and tell him how tired she was.

To her surprise, Tobias pulled away from the kiss. He looked into Tracy's eyes. "I am sorry. I know that you need more from me as a boyfriend." He shrugged. "I want to give you more. I want to be the man that you need. Not because of the pressure Mackenzie and the world are putting us. I want to be better for you. I want to be a better boyfriend because I don't want to lose you." For the first time since she had known him, Tracy saw fear in the eyes of the man whom she had thought to be fearless. Tobias shifted his eyes to the floor and then back to Tracy. "I love you. I don't want to lose you, but I am afraid that my inability to know what to do is going to push you away from me." Tobias walked over to the bed and slumped down onto it. "I am exhausted and I know that you are too. I want to talk about how I can be better, but right now, I really need some sleep. I am sorry to dump this on you and then say I need to rest." Tobias shrugged. "I just don't think I could have slept unless I let you know how I feel and that I want to make this work. That I want to be with you. Tomorrow, can you and I just talk about how I can be better without therapists or Mackenzie or the president around, watching us like we are some kind of a soap opera?'"

Tracy's eyes began to well up with tears as she walked over toward the bed. She placed her arms around Tobias and she shifted his face toward hers. She kissed him and then placed her forehead on his and looked into his eyes. "I love you too. Tomorrow, we can talk about how we can both be better. I have to work at being better too."

The two lovers shared one more long kiss then they laid back down on their bed, holding each other in their arms. For the first time since she had awkwardly approached Tobias and expressed her feelings toward him, she felt as if there was a chance they might have a future together.

THE ATLANTIC OCEAN

The long and winding trunk of the inexplicable cryptid probed the ocean floor. Trunko's appendage acted like a huge vacuum cleaner, sucking up any and all tiny forms of life on the ocean floor. Shrimp, krill, plankton, small crabs, starfish, and various forms of small bottom-feeding fish were sucked up into the monster's trunk. Once the long, white, fur-covered trunk was full of food, the monster curled the tip of the appendage back toward his face and emptied its contents into his mouth.

Trunko reached his long trunk down to the ocean floor to repeat this process when his acute sense of smell alerted him to a possible threat. When he was at his original size, only the largest oceanic predators such as orcas, sperm whales, and the occasional large great white shark presented any threat to the fur-covered monster. Since he had undergone the change that had caused him to grow to his current size, Trunko had not experienced any form of attack. The scent that he detected was similar to that of the great white sharks that had threatened him in his past life. This scent was different though. The scent of the sharks that were now approaching him were as different from the scent from the sharks of his past as his own scent was from before he had grown. The realization that a potential threat was moving toward him activated Trunko's fight or flight response. The monster began to swim in a tight circle just above the ocean's floor. As he swam, Trunko began to slam his fluke-like tail and his long trunk into the ocean floor. In his previous life, Trunko was a timid creature. The cryptid would typically flee from a threat, but like all creatures that had been subjected to Rol-Hama's alterations, Trunko's rage and aggressive tendencies were now uninhibited. The monster continued to slam his tail and trunk into the ocean floor until he worked himself up into a frenzy. The cryptid trumpeted out a battle cry and then began swimming toward the two oncoming MEGs.

****

Tracy slept for nearly ten hours. When she finally woke up, she saw Tobias sitting up in bed next to her, watching the news. Tracy rolled over to see the CNN news anchor and her panel discussing the current state of the world economic and geopolitical crisis that was occurring as a result of a total stoppage on cross-oceanic shipping. Shipping across the oceans was the first link in the long chain of worldwide commerce that helped society to function as it currently did. The young doctor sat up in bed and placed her hand in Tobias' just as one of the panel showed an idiot-proof diagram that explained just how dire the situation was. The chart showed how without ships bringing new fuel to the U.S., Great Britain, France, and other countries that relied on it, not only were individual people being limited on the amount of travel they could do but so were things like trucking companies. With shipping companies unable to fuel their trucks adequately, large shipments of food were only able to reach a quarter of their normal deliveries. This was resulting in a food shortage that was causing long lines and riots as people were panicking about being able to feed their families.

The panel member was about to start discussing other effects of the shipping crisis when Tobias turned to Tracy. "This is on us. We need to figure things out and get the MEGs out there to kill these monsters and get the world back on track."

Tracy took a deep breath as she realized that the time for the first of many talks she and Tobias needed have was here. She turned off the TV and placed her hand on Tobias' shoulder. "This is one of the issues that I have. I don't how to be a good girlfriend, or significant other, or whatever we are at this point. Social skills have always been something that I have lacked. Being a girlfriend is difficult enough for me." She sighed. "I am a scientist. When dealing with an issue, I need to eliminate as many variables as possible. Being a good girlfriend is a variable with a lot attached to it. When I add on the fact that the world is falling apart because of my inability to understand your feelings and express my own, it makes this entire situation more than I can handle. I need to separate working on our relationship from the fate of the world in order to be successful at it."

Tobias nodded. "I can't do that. I am a pilot, a soldier. It's my job to protect the world. Everyday, Mackenzie, the news, people that I pass in the hallway, remind me of how the world is depending on me to save it. When I was in the Air Force, it was so much easier. I had clearly defined missions and targets. When I was synced with ROC 1, all I had to do was to take out the next giant cryptid. Even when ROC 1 died, my mission was still simple. All that I had to do was find and take out Rol-Hama." He grabbed Tracy's hand. "This, us being a couple, is so much more difficult for me. I've never had someone who I cared about, who I loved, on a mission with me. I mean, of course I would have given up my life to protect any of my fellow pilots when I was on a mission. That's what you sign up for when you enlist. With you, it's something different. If you lose a friend on a mission, it's what you expect. It's what you prepare for. In order to minimize the impact on yourself, you shut down as many emotions as you can. When you lose someone in the line of duty, you honor their sacrifice and remember them for their bravery. Then you move on because if you don't have yourself in the right mindset because you are focused on those you lost, more people will die. With you, I can't think that way. In the short time we have been together, you have meant more to me than I can say. For the first time, I can't stand the thought of losing someone. I can't stand the thought of losing you."

Tobias squeezed her hand tighter. "When you are in the field, the mission comes before anything else. Sometimes, you can see a friend or fellow pilot is going to die. If you can save them, you save them. However, if saving them will endanger the mission, your first priority is the mission. I can't bring myself to think that way with you. I am afraid if it comes down to it, that if we are in a situation where MEG 1 is in danger and you can't disconnect in order to preserve the mission, I am afraid that I will choose to save you over the mission."

He shook his head. "I know if I lose you, I will be emotionally compromised. Then it's compounded by the fact that not just more people will die, but hundreds of thousands, if not millions, of people will die. They'll die slow and painful deaths. They won't be shot and die on the spot like a soldier. They'll die from starving to death, from not getting the medicine they need, from God knows what else." The pilot shrugged. "They'll all die because I can't stand losing you." Tobias looked into her eyes. "The most frustrating part of this entire situation is that all of these issues can be improved if I am simply able to continue to make progress in our relationship. God help me, I'm not sure how to do that."

Tracy fought back tears as she leaned in and kissed him. "I don't know how either, but I think today we took a step in the right direction."

The two lovers were holding each other when a red light started flashing throughout their room. The flashing light was accompanied by a blaring siren. When he first heard the alarm, Tobias jumped out of bed and immediately started getting dressed. Tracy was still not fully awake and she wasn't sure what the alarm meant until she heard Jillian's voice over the intercom system. "Captain Crow and Dr. Curry, report to the neurolink room immediately! This is not a drill! Repeat, this not a drill."

Tobias was nearly dressed when Tracy finally got out of bed. She started putting her clothes on as she looked over at Tobias. "What does she mean, this not a drill?"

Tobias turned around and looked Tracy in the eye. "It means the MEGs are going to be put into battle sooner than we thought."

Tracy shook her head. "I thought Jillian said that we had almost twenty-four hours until we had to engage Trunko?"

Tobias shrugged. "Sometimes, the enemy doesn't work on the timetable you want them to." Tobias knelt down and quickly tied his shoes. He was fully ready to go when he looked at Tracy to see her standing with a shirt on and no pants. Tracy was just staring at the wall as the realization that she was going to take MEG 1 into battle for the first time dawned on her.

Tobias reached out and grabbed her hand. "Tracy, we have to get moving. We have to sync with the MEGs now! Before something engages them without us being connected to them."

Tracy nodded and then she started to get dressed as quickly as she could. Once she was fully dressed, the two MEG pilots sprinted out of their quarters toward the neurolink. As Tracy was running, she was both terrified and relieved at the same time. She had dreaded the first time she was going to pilot MEG 1 in a combat situation. Tracy was a doctor and a healer. She had never so much as been in a fist fight in her entire life. Tobias was a lifelong warrior. He had been in countless close-quarter fights, shootouts, and aerial dogfights long before he ever piloted ROC 1. Tobias knew how to fight. Tracy had no idea what to do in a fight. She was also still struggling to increase her ability to sync with MEG 1, and to not freak out when sharing a mind with the giant shark.

Ever since Mackenzie had first told her that she would be the pilot for MEG 1, Tracy had wondered how much help she would be in guiding the hybrid beast through a physical confrontation. The thought had been rolling around in the back of her mind even as she did her best not to think about it. Hours ago, when she was told she would pilot MEG 1 into battle against Trunko, she had been worried about what she would do in a fight.

As she ran into the neurolink room, she was partly relieved that she would no longer have the stress weighing her down of what to do in a battle, because the battle was here.

Jillian Crean and Mackenzie were sitting at the computer consoles that were connected to the neurolink. As Tobias ran by them, he shouted out, "What happened to move up the timetable?"

Mackenzie looked up from his screen and yelled, "Trunko must have sensed the MEGs coming toward him. He started swimming north a couple of hours ago. At first, we thought he was just going about his normal movements. After an hour of swimming straight toward the MEGs, it was pretty clear he was moving to engage them."

Mackenzie pointed to the neurolink recliners. "Get yourselves synced up with the MEGs. I'll send all of the information we have on the target through the link."

Tobias nodded, jumped into his recliner, and quickly placed the neurolink helmet over his head.

Tracy stopped as she stood above her neurolink recliner. She looked toward Tobias and when she saw that he was already synced with MEG 2, her head snapped the other way to look at Jillian Crean. Jillian knew her friend was looking for some kind of reassurance. Jillian stood and ran over to her friend. She hugged Tracy and said, "You can do this. Mackenzie and I will be following along through the link and Tobias will be right there next to you."

Mackenzie yelled out, "Five minutes until the target reaches the MEGs! Sync with MEG 1 now before her instincts take over and make it impossible for you to engage with her." Tracy let go of her friend and did her best to let go of her fears as well as she climbed into her recliner and pulled the neurolink helmet over her head.

There was a bright flash of light in front of Tracy's eyes, and then a moment later, she saw nothing but dark blue water in front of her. Through MEG 1's electroreception senses, she could feel something massive swimming toward her. She was trying her best to understand the scope of the monster when text started running across her field of vision. Tracy still wasn't used to the sensation of Mackenzie and Jillian being able to type directions directly into her mind. Every time a message suddenly appeared before her eyes, it startled her a little. Her brief loss of concentration caused her sync with MEG 1 to weaken. When the shark felt Tracy's influence backing away from her, the beast began to thrash from side to side.

Tracy took a deep breath. She then refocused her thoughts first on MEG 1 to reassure the shark that she was there. Once the shark had calmed down, Tracy focused on the text that was scrolling before her eyes.

Trunko is two hundred and eighty feet long. He is extremely dense and muscular. This cryptid is both heavier and stronger than either of the MEGs. Trunko has two flippers on the side of his body and a fluke-like tail. He also has the elephant-like trunk from which he gets his name. It is unknown if the monster has gills, lungs, or some combination of both. Hit and run is the recommended attack plan.

MEG 1 slowed down her approach as Tracy was trying to figure out how to best execute a "hit and run" attack on a monster. She was still considering her attack plan when she saw a stark white form moving toward her in the darkness. As a child, she had watched the old Gregory Peck version of Moby Dick. The sight of the great white whale moving through the water to attack Ahab's ship had terrified her. Tracy felt a quick jolt of fear run down her spine. She was trying to find a way to work through her fear when she saw MEG 2 dart past her as he swam toward Trunko.

Trunko bellowed loudly when he saw MEG 2 streaking toward him. The white beast had been charging the larger MEG 1, but when he saw the male shark swimming toward him, Trunko altered his course to meet the oncoming threat.

Despite being only two-thirds the size of the cryptid, MEG 2 swam directly at Trunko. Just before he reached the monster, Tobias had MEG 2 shift to the side and swim past the cryptid's outstretched trunk. Once he was clear of the trunk, MEG 2 shifted his body back toward Trunko and used his diamond-coated steel fin to slice into the monster's side. Trunko shook his head back and forth as blood poured out of his side. MEG 2 had managed to create a long cut on the side of the creature, but the wound was only superficial. Trunko's thick musculature had prevented the shark's fin from reaching any organs or vital tissues.

Tracy was mesmerized by the size of the leviathan before her, and the speed and agility of MEG 2. She was so enthralled by what she was looking at that she didn't realize MEG 1 was still swimming directly toward Trunko.

She saw the words, *DIVE! DIVE!* flash in front of her eyes. She looked through the words to see the monster's powerful white trunk reaching out for her like a huge tentacle. Trunko wrapped his trunk around MEG 1's gills, cutting off her ability to breathe. The cryptid then began pushing the shark backward and down toward the ocean floor.

MEG 1 instinctively began biting into Trunko's head, but even the giant shark's jaws were unable to penetrate the cryptid's thick skull. Tracy's human body began to shake as MEG 1 was suffocating. The young doctor was starting to panic and through the neurolink, MEG 1 felt that panic. The sense of panic caused the shark to stop biting the cryptid and to try and break away from it. MEG 1 tried to pull away from Trunko, but the shark's panicked actions only caused the monster's grip on her gills to tighten.

Tobias could see that MEG 1 was in trouble. He quickly turned MEG 2 around and charged Trunko. When he reached the monster, MEG 2 dove beneath Trunko and used his dorsal fin slice into the monster's belly. MEG 2 turned around to see a cloud of blood oozing out of Trunko's stomach, but this cut also proved to be superficial.

Tobias watched as MEG 1 continued to struggle to free herself from Trunko's grip. The pilot knew that he needed to change tactics and act quickly if he was to save MEG 1 and possibly Tracy from dying. MEG 2 streaked toward Trunko and sank his teeth into Trunko's fluke-like tail. MEG 2 shook his head from side to side in an attempt to tear off the monster's tail. Tobias was surprised when, with one flick of his tail, the powerful cryptid shook MEG 2 free of his fluke and sent the shark tumbling through the water.

Back in the neurolink room, Tracy Curry's body started to convulse. Jillian Crean looked over at Mackenzie. "She feels as if she's being strangled. We need to disconnect her now or she is going to die!"

Jillian stood up to disconnect her friend from the neurolink when Mackenzie shouted at her, "Sit down! If we lose MEG 1 now, this entire mission is a failure. We need to get Curry back in control of herself and MEG 1 or the entire world is screwed!"

Mackenzie began furiously typing commands through the neurolink. *Electric Discharge! Calm down! Focus on someone special and think about what they mean to you. Then use your Electric Discharge!*

Tracy saw the words scrolling in front of her. It took her panicked mind a few seconds to understand what the words meant. When she finally realized the command she was being given, she focused first on Tobias and her growing feelings toward him. The thought of Tobias calmed her. She then switched her focus to MEG 1 and instructed her to unleash a burst of electricity.

Thousands of volts of electricity danced around MEG 1's body and poured into Trunko. The massive cryptid bellowed in pain as the attack shocked him, but the monster's trunk remained fixed around the shark's gills.

Tracy's body stopped convulsing as she regained control of herself. She clenched her teeth and continued to send wave after wave of electricity through MEG 1 and into Trunko.

Through MEG 2's eyes, Tobias could see that the electrical attack was hurting Trunko. He had MEG 2 swim up next to Trunko and bite into the monster's flipper. Once MEG 2 had the flipper trapped within his teeth, Tobias had the shark press his body against Trunko's side and add his own electrical attack to MEG 1's.

Trunko's body was racked with pain as shock after shock assaulted him. The monster realized he needed to move away from the MEGs if he wanted to survive. Trunko released his grip on MEG 1's gills and the massive shark was immediately able to breathe again.

Tracy could see that Trunko was trying to swim away from MEG 1 and she urged the shark to swim forward and bite into his trunk. For the first time, Tracy was synced with MEG 1 as fresh blood filled the shark's mouth. The young doctor could feel the rush of adrenaline that ran through MEG 1 as the monster tasted flesh. The sensation both scared and invigorated Tracy at the same time. She suddenly found herself obsessed with killing Trunko. MEG 1 felt Tracy's desire to slay the monster and in response to Tracy's emotions, MEG 1 tore the cryptid's trunk off his face. A cloud of blood gushed out of the monster's face and surrounded MEG 1. The scent of blood pushed MEG 1 deeper into a feeding frenzy. The colossal shark darted forward and bit hard onto the gaping wound where the cryptid's trunk had been torn from his face.

Tracy's hands clenched into fists as she directed MEG 1 to continue to send electric shocks into Trunko.

The cryptid struggled to break free as the two MEGs continued to send wave after wave of electricity into him. The monster experienced several minutes of agonizing pain before his heart finally gave out. When they were sure that Trunko was dead, the MEGs stopped shocking the monster. MEG 2 swam away from the monster and then he spun around and darted toward the dead Trunko with his jaws wide open. MEG 2 slammed into Trunko's side and began tearing at the monster's thick muscles until he tore a piece of it off and devoured it.

Tracy was watching through MEG 1's eyes and she felt the shark's primal urge to feast on the carcass of the dead beast. Tracy's human body began salivating as MEG 1 closed in on the monster's corpse. MEG 1 was just about to take a bite out of Trunko when Tracy saw a bright flash of light and found herself back in the neurolink room looking up at Tobias.

Tobias looked down at her and said, "You don't want to be connected to them when they are feeding if you can help it. You will feel their urges now, but you will feel your own sense of disgust later."

Tracy nodded as she kept her eyes fixed on Tobias. Her body still felt excited from the sensations she had experienced from MEG 1. MEG 1 needed to feed, but Tracy needed something else. She needed some other way to expel the energy that was surging through her body. She stood up, grabbed Tobias, and kissed him. Tracy kissed him long and hard, pressing her body against his in the process. When she finally broke the kiss, she looked toward Jillian and Mackenzie. "We have a while until we need to sync with the MEGs again, right?"

The CIA director and Tracy's best friend had seen what happened to the first set of pilots after they had engaged in a battle while synced with the ROCs. The pilots' emotions were running on overdrive from sharing a mind with a monster that was fighting for its life. The pilots' minds seemed to steer their emotions from fear and anger to other emotions that were easier for them to deal with and placate.

Mackenzie nodded. "The MEGs will be feeding on Trunko's thick hide for a while. Then it will be a few hours before they reach their next target. Why don't you two go and get some R and R?"

Tracy didn't respond. She simply grabbed Tobias' hand and started sprinting back to their quarters. Tracy pulled Tobias into their bedroom and she kissed him again before tearing off his shirt and pulling off hers. She then pushed Tobias onto the bed and jumped on top of him.

CHAPTER 7
U.S. NAVAL BASE DIEGO GARCIA, INDIAN OCEAN

Raphael Clark's alarm woke him up at five am to start his maintenance duties on the naval base. He rolled over in his bed to see the first rays of sunlight peeking in through a nearby window. He walked over to the window and opened it to see the sun as it began to ascend over the ocean.

He took a deep breath to savor the salt air. He was slightly surprised that there seemed to be an odd musky smell that was tainting the usually refreshing smell of the ocean. He shrugged. "Must be something rotting in the surf off the island." He then closed the window so that the smell would stay out of the building.

The young sailor had only joined the Navy a year ago. Raphael had enlisted right before Rol-Hama unleashed an army of giant cryptids on the world and changed everything. Raphael had spent his entire tenure at the remote Diego Garcia Base, making minor repairs and conducting routine maintenance on the ships there. Due to the fact that his post kept him more or less stationary, he had avoided any conflict with the giant cryptids. Raphael was no coward, but he was not eager to die either. From what he had heard, the monsters that had first attacked cities across the planet were dead and now a new group of monsters were attacking ships on all four oceans.

It was because of these attacks that the president had ordered all ocean-going traffic to come to a halt. The entire U.S. Naval fleet was now docked and awaiting orders to see if a new classified attack plan would be able to destroy the sea monsters that currently ruled the oceans. As a result of all the ships being docked, Diego Garcia had nearly three times the number of ships that it would typically hold on a given day. Three times the number of ships docked at the base meant three times the amount of maintenance that Raphael and his crew would typically perform. The last he had heard, the tracker on the monster in the Indian Ocean had it near Diego Garcia. The fact that the fleet might need to be mobilized quickly had the base on high alert. The high alert also meant that Raphael and his crew needed to address any maintenance problems as quickly as possible so the ships were able to set sail at a moment's notice.

Raphael quickly showered, shaved, and dressed himself then he grabbed his tools and jogged out to the first ship he was going to work on. The *USS Alaska* was a massive aircraft carrier. According to its captain, the plumbing system for the toilets on the ship wasn't working correctly and they were backing up. Raphael was not looking forward to examining the septic system for a ship that was the size of a city block and held nearly that many people, but orders were orders. When he approached the *Alaska*, the musky smell grew stronger. Raphael shook his head. "If that smell is coming from the backed-up pipes, we need to take a look at what the boys on that ship have been eating."

As Raphael was walking out on the dock to the huge carrier, he knelt down to check the bottom of the ship's hull. One of the main reasons for a ship's toilets backing up was if coral or some other form of sea life had formed on the pipes that emptied the toilets into the ocean. Raphael saw a huge wad of brown massed around the hull of the ship just below the water line. He shook his head. "Damnit. Looks like a ton of kelp is stuck down there. I am going to have to move that out of the way before I can even check the exterior pipes."

Raphael was staring at the kelp, trying to figure out the best way to remove it from the hull of the ship, when the seemingly massed plant life began to shift away from the *Alaska*. Raphael stood up and winced. "That's odd. The current shouldn't be strong enough to move that much kelp at low tide." He moved closer to the end of the dock. When he looked down into the water at what he thought was kelp, Raphael screamed.

Looking back at him through the water was a face that was an odd mix of an orangutan and a human. The face rose out of the ocean as the monster which had been crouched down and lurking beneath the water stood up. A mixture of saltwater and thick brown fur fell down onto Raphael, and it quickly became apparent where the strange musky smell was originating from. The volume of water hitting the sailor was enough to knock him off the dock and into the ocean.

The naval mechanic swam back to the surface of the water to see the full height and form of the monster that had risen from the depths. Raphael had seen pictures of the giant Sasquatch who had ravaged the U.S. west coast the previous year. In general appearance, this monster resembled that creature, but there were subtle differences. While the Sasquatch was muscular with a broad chest and wide shoulders, this creature was more slim and athletic looking. Another difference was the hands of the two monsters. The Sasquatch had hands that looked like a human or some kind of an ape. This monster had recognizable hands but more than an ape's hands, they reminded Raphael of the clawed hands of a werewolf from a movie.

The monster looked down at Raphael and then he turned toward the *Alaska* and shrieked. The hairy creature then turned and began tearing into the carrier with his claws. For a brief moment, Raphael looked up at the creature and remembered tales that sailors who had been to Japan and China had told him of the Shojo. As best as Raphael could remember, the Shojo was kind of an ape-man that lived under the ocean. The legend was mostly associated with drunken sailors because the idea of an ape-man living underwater was insane. As Raphael had to swim to his left to avoid falling debris from the *Alaska*, he knew that the Shojo was all too real.

Raphael swam back to the shore and climbed out of the water. He then turned around to see that the Shojo had torn apart the entire front half of the *Alaska*. The back half of the ship was quickly filling up with water and slipping beneath the waves as the Shojo shrieked and turned to the ship next to it. A deafening boom shook the sky above Raphael. He looked up to see two surface-to-air missiles streaking toward the aquatic ape. The missiles slammed into the ape-man's chest and exploded. The entire top half of the Shojo's body was engulfed in flames and Raphael cheered, thinking the monster had been slain.

Raphael's cheers changed to gasps when the wind blew the smoke away to reveal that the Shojo was uninjured from the assault. Raphael crawled to shore as jeeps and trucks pulled up to the waterline with sailors carrying everything from handguns to bazookas. The sailors fired on the Shojo as helicopters flew overhead and added their own fury to the assault. The Shojo was lit up by a barrage of missiles and bullets, but the might of the U.S. Navy could do nothing to slow the monster's onslaught. The Shojo waded through the water toward the next ship. The beast ignored the firepower that was striking him as if it were nothing more than a gentle breeze.

The man-beast lifted his long dagger-like claws into that air and then he raked the side of the *USS Winslow*. Eight massive gouges were torn into the ship as the Shojo's claws cut through it. The troops on land continued their ineffective barrage as another wave of sailors ran to ships that were still intact and docked with the hopes of using their larger weapons on the monster.

Raphael watched as sailors poured onto the *USS Margate*. The ship was to the right of the of the sunken *Alaska* and in the opposite direction of the way the monster was moving. Raphael hoped that the ground and air forces could keep the Shojo distracted long enough for the *Margate* to maneuver into a position where it could attack the beast.

For a moment, Raphael watched as the Shojo tore a huge chunk out of the *Winslow* and lifted it over his head. The monster shrieked once more, and then he tossed the several-ton hunk of crushed metal at the sailors who were firing on him from the shore. The chunk of the destroyed ship flew through the air and created a huge shadow that covered most of the people who were attacking the Shojo. Raphael reacted quickly and ran toward the water in order to avoid the falling debris. When his feet reentered the harbor, he turned around to see the debris fall onto over twenty sailors, instantly crushing them to death.

The sailors who were still alive on the beach were covered in a wave of sand from the impact of the debris. Raphael could see sailors trying to dig themselves out from the sand when two Apache helicopters flew over the buried sailors and began firing on the Shojo. The helicopters chain-gun bullets soared through the sky like miniature white-hot lasers. The bullets struck the Shojo, but like all other attacks thus far, they had not managed to injure the monster. Like two moons orbiting a planet, the twin Apaches took a position circling the Shojo as they continued to fire upon the creature. The monster shook off the high-caliber bullets as he pulled another chunk off the wrecked *Winslow.* The Shojo ripped a long, thick strip of steel off the ship and then he swung it like a colossal club at the circling Apaches. The first helicopter was crushed before its pilot had a chance to react. The second one was pulling away from the Shojo when the monster turned and batted it out of the air with his club.

Raphael was still standing in the water and staring at the Shojo in utter disbelief of the monster's power and fury. He looked to his right to see the *Margate* now in the middle of the harbor facing the monster. Raphael knew what was coming next, and he quickly ran back to shore. When he reached the beach, the maintenance man kept moving away from the water until he was standing next to the chunk of the debris that had crushed the ground forces mere moments ago.

Raphael looked back toward the ocean to see two objects moving quickly through the water between the *Margate* and the Shojo. He jumped behind the chunk of debris that now served as a gravestone for many of his friends and he put his hands over his ears. Raphael had his back placed against the huge chunk of metal when there was a deafening explosion followed by a shockwave that shook the entire beach. Sand and water blew past the debris Raphael was hiding behind. The sand and water were followed by a wave of heat that heated the debris Raphael was leaning against to the point that it burned his skin. Raphael closed his eyes and rolled away from the burning metal. He took several deep breaths and then he opened his eyes and looked back toward the harbor to see the Shojo wadding out toward the *Margate.*

The *Margate* began firing its main gun at the Shojo, but Raphael knew the gun was no match for the monster. The destroyer had hit the Shojo with two torpedoes that could have obliterated a nuclear submarine and the monster was unfazed by the attack. Raphael watched as the Shojo dove beneath the water in front of the *Margate.* The monster resurfaced next to the ship and placed his claws along its starboard side. With one push, the Shojo capsized the *Margate.* The once-mighty ship was floating helplessly on its side with its hull facing the monster. The Shojo shrieked and then raked his claws across the hull of the ship, tearing huge gashes into it. Raphael could see numerous sailors leaping into the water, but he knew that most of the brave crew would be trapped within the ship and drown to death.

As the *Margate* filled with water and started to sink into the sea, the Shojo began wadding back to the other docked ships. The monster swam to the nearest carrier and began ripping it pieces. More sailors came running onto the beach, but this time, they didn't attack the monster. They just stood there next to Raphael and watched as the Shojo continued to attack the ship.

Raphael turned to one of the sailors. "What's the next plan of attack?"

The sailor shrugged. "The ROCs are in the air and should be here within thirty minutes. Until then, the admiral's orders are to stand down. He says that we hit the monster with our most powerful weapons and it didn't even slow him down. It seems like the monster is content to stay in the water and attack the ships. The admiral figures the ships are going down no matter what and it's better if we don't lose more sailors in the process of trying to defend them. Our job is to now watch what the monster is doing and do our best to document it."

Raphael nodded and looked back at the Shojo as it finished destroying one ship and moved to the next. The Shojo sank two more ships before several of the sailors started shouting out orders for everyone to clear the beach.

When Raphael saw everyone else running toward the barracks, he joined in with them. He had only managed to run roughly a hundred yards when he saw a colossal object moving across the horizon toward him. He briefly caught the image of a giant bird with metal wings before it blocked out the sun and cast the entire base into shadow. At the sight of the approaching ROC 2, one of the sailors yelled. "Down on the ground, and cover your ears!"

Raphael dropped to the ground, covered his ears, and then he rolled so that he was facing the harbor. He could see the Shojo standing in waist-deep water and attacking another carrier as ROC 2 streaked toward it at what seemed like a quickly increasing speed. When ROC 2 was directly over the Shojo, the giant cybernetic bird shattered the sound barrier and created a sonic boom. The force of the sonic boom shook the entire island and staggered the Shojo, causing the beast to fall backward into the water.

As the Shojo was trying to regain his senses beneath the water, ROC 2 swerved around and began circling above him. The Shojo shook his head and then exploded out the water with his claws reaching for ROC 2. ROC 2 flew away from monster, firing her diamond-coated steel feathers at the creature as she did so. The deadly feathers pierced the Shojo's seemingly indestructible hide and caused the monster to bleed for the first time. Enraged and in pain, the Shojo shrieked and began making his way toward ROC 2. ROC 2 continued to back up as the Shojo wadded toward her, but the cyborg did not fly away from the monster.

Raphael was wondering why ROC 2 didn't take off into the sky to put some distance between herself and the Shojo when the island was suddenly covered in darkness again. The maintenance man looked up to see ROC 4 flying toward the battle. When ROC 2 saw ROC 4 streaking toward the Shojo, the giant bird quickly increased her altitude. The Shojo shrieked at the retreating ROC 2 as ROC 4 quickly increased his speed over the sea beast and struck him with a second sonic boom.

The force of the blast once more knocked the Shojo beneath the waves and sent millions of gallons of water flying into the air. The Shojo was briefly knocked unconscious from the blast until his head struck the ocean floor. The monster's eyes snapped open and he turned around to see ROC 2 and ROC 4 circling in the air above the water. The Shojo growled at the cybernetic birds, but the command that was constantly running through his head was telling him to attack ships and other oceanic installations, not to fight with giant birds. The Shojo growled once more, then he pressed his body as close to the ocean floor as he could and began swimming back out to deeper water.

Raphael watched as the two ROCs flew over the ocean, following the Shojo until he lost sight of them over the horizon.

When the ROCs were out of sight, Raphael and the other sailors slowly began to stand up. One of the other soldiers walked up to Raphael and tried to talk to him, but the maintenance man's ears were still ringing from the sonic booms given off by the ROCs. From what he could make out from the way the other sailor's mouth was moving, Raphael guessed he was saying, "Are your ears ringing too?"

Raphael nodded in reply to the sailor who replied in kind and then pointed back to the barracks. Raphael turned and began walking back to the barracks. He was halfway to the barracks and ready to make his report when he stopped and looked back at the harbor to see the remains of at least five ships poking out of the water. The sailor who had asked him if his ears were ringing stopped and looked back as well.

Raphael still heard a ringing in his ears, but he guessed his hearing was clearing up when he heard the sailor talking. "That monster took out nearly a quarter of the ships stationed in the Indian Ocean in under an hour and we couldn't do a thing to stop him!" The sailor shook his head. "How are we going to stop that thing from taking out every other base on the planet?"

Raphael shrugged. "All I know is that there is some kind of new attack plan. Let's go in and tell the officers what we saw. Hopefully, it can help out with the new plan and prevent this from happening again." The other sailor nodded in reply and then the two men silently entered the barracks.

****

Back at the NEST, David Bixby and Lindsay Munroe were lying in their neurolink recliners next to each other. They kept their recliners close enough so that they could hold hands while they were synced with the ROCs. The young lovers had found being in physical contact with each other helped them to better focus on their feelings for each other and through those emotions build a stronger sync with the ROCs.

The pilots stayed linked with the ROCs as they followed the signal being given off by the Shojo's tracker. The two monstrous birds circled the water above where the Shojo was for hours, waiting for the demon to resurface, but the beast remained below the waves. Eventually, the ROCs reached the point where they needed to return to land to rest and eat. The pilots had the cybernetic guardians returned to their temporary base in Africa, and then they removed their neurolinks.

The briefly looked at each other and kissed passionately before saying anything. When they finally broke off their kiss, Bixby looked at Munroe. "I don't know if that thing is going to surface again now that he's seen what's waiting for him."

Munroe nodded. "Yeah, it's going to be up to Crow and Curry to take that thing down with the MEGs."

They were both climbing out of there recliners when Bixby gave Munroe a worried look. "That thing was no pushover. Do you think that Crow and Curry will be able to form a deep enough bond with the MEGs to beat it?" Bixby shrugged. "Hell, the MEGs aren't even as developed as the ROCs. Do you think even if they have a strong enough sync that the MEGs are going to be able to kill that ape?"

Munroe shrugged. "I honestly don't know Curry too well, but we both know Crow. He can do anything that he puts his mind too. It's a matter of him taking that skill and applying it to his heart."

CHAPTER 8
BALTIMORE

After the better part of an hour's worth of working off the energy from their last sync with the MEGs, Tracy rolled over and looked into Tobias' eyes. She took a few deep breaths before she started talking. "I know syncing with the MEGs can have an effect on our emotions, but I have never felt so overcome with, let's just call it desire, after one of our past syncs with the MEGs."

Tobias nodded. "The emotional feedback through the link is much stronger after a battle. It can be almost overwhelming. The best I can figure, our brains are smart enough to take all of the anger we feel from the monsters and direct it toward some other emotion."

Tracy nodded. "How did you deal with the emotions after syncing with ROC 1? I mean, I know how Bixby and Munroe dealt with it, but how did you deal with those emotions?"

Tobias shook his head. "I guess I didn't deal with them. I mean, for the most part, I dominated ROC 1's consciousness, so I blocked out as much of his emotions as I could. Still, some of it would seep through. After each battle, I felt even more focused and determined to kill all the cryptids Rol-Hama had unleashed. I would then focus that energy on working out or researching whatever I could on the monsters we were fighting." He shrugged. "At first, I thought that approach was a good thing. I thought it was pushing me to complete the mission, but in reality, what it was doing was pushing me away from ROC 1."

Tobias sighed. "I told you before, I had never really had a meaningful relationship with anyone. My family was never a caring one. We just all sort of existed together. I never really felt like a part of anything until I joined the military." He looked toward Tracy. "I know you could sense how uncomfortable it was for me to look at the sea ape or whatever it was because it reminded me of the Sasquatch that killed ROC 1."

Tracy kissed his forehead. "I know you experienced the sensation of ROC 1 dying. We were barely able to break your link with him before he died. That would be difficult for anyone to overcome."

Tobias shook his head. "It was more than just feeling what it was like for ROC 1 to die. It was feeling what it was like for him to die alone. He died without feeling any connection to another creature on this planet. The closest thing he had to a connection with anyone was with me and I left him as he was dying."

He looked at Tracy. "It was that feeling. That sensation of absolutely knowing what it would be like to die alone that helped me to express my feelings for you." He shook his head. "Does that make me a bad person? That I needed this magnificent creature who wanted to connect with me and who I blocked out to die to realize I need other people in my life? That I need someone to care for me and to have someone I care about?"

Tracy hugged Tobias. "You knew ROC 1 better than anyone else. He was part of you just as you were a part of him. What did he feel when he died? Was it just fear and sadness or was there something else?"

Crow began to tear up. "He didn't feel any fear or sadness. I don't know if it was because I was in his mind for so long or if it was just innately within him, but he thought that he died doing his duty. In those last few seconds, I don't know if it was his feelings or mine, but I think he was happy when he felt me being pulled out his mind. Almost as if he was glad that I was being saved. The thing is, I don't know if those were my thoughts or his and I don't know if I should feel grateful or guilty to have them."

Tracy hugged him harder. "Those thoughts were ROC 1's. I know that because I am getting to know you. I have seen you stare death in the face multiple times without blinking. You are not afraid to die for something you believe in and neither was ROC 1. He didn't die alone. He died knowing that you, the one creature he did care about, was going to live."

Tobias shook his head and Tracy pulled back and looked him in the eye. "How did you feel today when you were synced with MEG 2? Did it feel different from your time with ROC 1 during the battle? Did it feel different after the battle?"

Tobias nodded. "I felt like the mission was priority, but I also felt that you and MEG 1 were priority. When I saw Trunko strangling you and MEG 1, I felt like all of the important things I was thinking about were connected. I felt that by focusing on you and on the mission, I was better able to work with MEG 2 to protect those things." He looked into Tracy's eyes. "Does that sound weird?"

She smiled. "No, it sounds exactly how I was starting to feel. When Trunko was strangling MEG 1, Jillian told me to think of someone I cared about and you were the first thing that came to mind. You were the person who gave me the strength to strengthen my bond with MEG 1 so together we could break free of Trunko's death grip." She smiled.

"While that was a pretty in-depth talk and it seems that we are syncing better with the MEGs, I guess at our next couples therapy session, we can tell the doctor we are making progress."

Tobias laughed. "Mackenzie is going to be pretty proud of us, isn't he?"

The still naked Tracy stood from the bed and started walking toward the shower. "Let's get showered off and then grab something to eat. We should still have a few hours until the MEGs reach the next target."

Tobias had a confused look on his face. "Wait, I still have to take you to dinner. Usually, I have to do that before…" He looked back at the bed and smiled. "You know."

Tracy threw a towel that hit him in the face. "Yes, Captain Crow, I plan to be more than just one of your *missions*. You are going to have to take me to dinner." She turned her head and looked seductively over her shoulder as she smiled. "That being said, I did say let's get a shower before going out, not showers plural." She walked into the bathroom and looked back at Tobias who eagerly followed her in.

****

George Mackenzie, Jillian Crean, and Rhonda Vaughn sat in the briefing room looking over the data from the MEGs battle with Trunko. Mackenzie shook his head as he looked at the readouts from Tracy's sync with MEG 1. "Curry almost lost it again. MEG 1 was almost strangled to death because she couldn't hold it together."

Crean leaned over and pointed to a section of data from later in the battle. "Yes, she struggled at first, but look at what happened later in the battle. She formed a stronger sync with MEG 1 than she ever has before. Once she reached this deeper state, she was able to handle the situation."

Mackenzie pushed the data aside. "Yes, she pulled through at the last minute, but is this always going to be the case? Is she going to need to be pushed to the brink of death before she gets her act together?"

Crean shrugged. "Bottom line, she got the job done. She is also showing progress in syncing with MEG 1. What else do you want from her?"

Mackenzie slammed his fist into the table. "I want her to be able to complete the mission she has been given. I want her to get her head on straight, learn how to function in a relationship, and make a strong connection with MEG 1. For Christ's sake, we still have four more sea monsters swimming around out there attacking ships that we need to take down!" He shifted his gaze over to Rhonda. "Dr. Vaughn, do you think that we can squeeze in another counseling session with them before their next mission?" He looked at his watch. "We have roughly three hours until the MEGs engage the Mermaid."

Dr. Vaughn shook her head. "One of the key parts of counseling any relationship is giving a couple time to reflect on and internalize the concepts discussed during our sessions. They are already averse to our sessions. I think that forcing them into another session will only serve to push them farther apart. Dr. Curry and Captain Crow simply need more time."

Mackenzie sighed in frustration. "Time is the one thing we don't have. The world is running out of supplies and crumbling around us with each passing second. We need Curry and Crow to be syncing with their MEGs at optimal efficiency now!"

Jillian started shouting as she leaned in closer to Mackenzie, "Damnit, George, they are making progress. If the data from the neurolink doesn't convince you of that, then take a look at how they are interacting with each other! You don't need to be a counselor to see that despite all of the pressure they are under, they are growing closer! Did you see how they took time to be with each other before the last briefing? They weren't just having sex, they were out jogging. They were enjoying a shared interest. They were working out stress together in a healthy manner! Have you noticed they have barely left each other's side since this whole thing began? Even for a couple in the honeymoon phase of a relationship, they are spending a lot of time together. Tracy and Tobias are doing fine." She leaned back in her chair. "Maybe to help put things in perspective, you should take a moment to think about how much quality time you've spent with your wife over the past year."

Mackenzie gritted his teeth and clenched his fists in anger. Crean had crossed a personal line, but she had made a valid point. He took a deep breath and loosened his fist. "All right, but they still almost lost MEG 1 during the last fight. Maybe we should have them resync with the MEGs and run one last training session as the sharks are en route to their next target."

Jillian shook her head. "No. They need some time away from the MEGs." She looked toward Rhonda. "It's just like Dr. Vaughn said when talking about how they are building their relationship. Tracy and Tobias need time to reflect on their last mission and internalize the information from it. Yes, they almost lost MEG 1, but the history of these two individuals indicates that defeat or near defeat is an experience they grow from." She softened her voice a little to try and better make her point to Mackenzie. "Tobias is a tactical genius in the field. Even if he is not overtly thinking about it, in his subconscious mind, he is running through what they did wrong in the battle with Trunko and how to avoid those mistakes next time. Throughout her life, Tracy has met and overcome every challenge she has faced. She may not always succeed at first, but she has proven she has the ability to learn from her mistakes and find a way to be successful."

Mackenzie stood up. "The only problem with that line of thinking is there are no second chances here. If we lose one MEG, the entire plan is finished. There is no way that MEG 2, even with Tobias Crow piloting him, can successfully complete this mission alone."

Mackenzie stood up. "I'll defer to the expertise of the two of you on this point. Let it be known though that I will be indicating in my report to the president that it was you two who pressed for this course of action. If the MEGs fail in their mission, you two can have it on your heads that the world is ending because you didn't want to push our pilots any harder."

Mackenzie stood up and started walking toward the door. When he grabbed the door handle, he stopped and turned around. "Crow and Curry can rest for two more hours, but I want them synced with the MEGs well before the sharks engage the Mermaid. I don't want them to be rushed into the sync right before battle like they were with Trunko." He sneered. "That's at least one part of getting them ready for their next battle that I can put my foot down about."

CHAPTER 9

After their time in the shower, Tracy and Tobias had each taken a short nap. They awoke to a see that it was a beautiful spring day outside. Tracy walked over to their window, opened it, took in a deep breath of fresh air, and then turned toward Tobias. "Good morning. It's too nice a day to spend it cooped up inside. I think that we still have some time before we need to sync up with the MEGs. What do you say to a quick jog, maybe once around the compound? Then we can eat and head to work to like a normal couple."

Tobias smiled. "Go to work like normal people. What *normal* people do you know that share a brain with a giant cybernetic animal and fight super-sized monsters?"

Tracy shrugged. "Bixby and Munroe?"

Tobias laughed. "I wouldn't exactly call those two normal. Do you know what they did after the first time they synced with the ROCs?"

Tracy winced. "No, I don't know, and I'm not sure I want to know."

Tobias smiled. "Yes, it's probably better if you don't know. Sharing your mind with a giant shark is tough enough but getting a peek into Bixby and Munroe's love life will really screw with your head."

Tracy laughed and then the two of them quickly put on shorts and T-shirts and stretched. The minutes later, they were jogging around the compound. As they were running, Tracy noticed that Tobias was not setting the usual strenuous pace that he typically did. She could see that something was on his mind and that he wanted to talk to her about it. Tracy smiled to herself at the fact that she was now able to realize when Tobias had something on his mind. She also felt she knew him well enough to understand that he would bring up whatever he was mulling over in his mind when he was ready too. Tracy kept quiet, but she made sure she was close enough to Tobias to hear him talk when he was ready.

They ran for another ten minutes when Tobias turned around to look at her. She could see that he was ready to say something, but she could also see whatever was on his mind was bothering him. The hardened Air Force pilot had a sheepish look on his face like a school boy who was going to ask a girl out for the first time. Tracy giggled at the look on his face and Tobias laughed as well.

The two of them stopped running and Tobias walked over to her. "What's so funny?"

Tracy laughed a little more. "You look like you have the most embarrassing thing in the world on your mind to say and you can't quite get it out."

Tobias smiled. "Am I that easy to read?"

Tracy smiled and nodded in reply.

Tobias shrugged. "It occurred to me that with everything going on, we have never really been on a date. Ever since Rol-Hama first unleashed giant cryptids on the world, we have either been training or in combat. In fact, we have hardly been off base in half a year."

Tracy calmed down when she realized that this was an opportunity to address an issue with Tobias she had been hesitant to bring up. She took a deep breath and tried to sound as reassuring as she could. "I have something in mind for us. I think it will be fun and maybe open you up to a new experience as well that can help with future challenges we might face. It's just something that might be a little out of your comfort zone."

Tobias shrugged "It's okay. I am sure that as long as you're there, I'll enjoy myself. What do you have in mind? Some kind of scientific lecture or something?"

Tracy blushed. "I was thinking we could go to a karaoke bar."

At the mention of singing karaoke, Tracy saw a look of true fear appear on Tobias' face. He shook his head. "Really? Me singing in front of all those people?"

Tracy nodded. "Look, I know that the newfound fame you acquired after flying ROC 1 and killing Rol-Hama was one of the more difficult issues you are struggling with. Everyone has things that make them uncomfortable and being in the spotlight is the thing that makes you uncomfortable. If we succeed in our new mission, the spotlight will be even brighter for you. The world is going to need a hero to look to as we rebuild, and who do you think they are going to look to? The president, the military, the news stations, they are all going to focus on you and what you have accomplished. You've fought monsters and killed crazed terrorists with your bare hands. No one is going to think that sticking a microphone in your face is going to be something you're afraid of, but I've seen you when the news is on or when the president congratulates you. Taking credit for your work, being in the spotlight, it's something you are afraid of and that's okay. It's normal. Everyone has fears, but as you know, we have to face them and overcome them."

She placed her arms around Tobias' neck. "Just like we have our fears, we also have our vices. For some people, it's smoking or drinking. For me, it's singing classic rock and country songs in front of a bar full of people." She smiled. "There's worse things to be addicted to. The reason I'm addicted to karaoke is that no matter how terrible of a singer you are, and trust me I suck, people always clap for you when you are done. When I was doing my graduate work, part of what it entailed was teaching a biology class to undergrads. Back then, I was terrified of public speaking and I all but froze up while teaching the first class. The person who was mentoring me through my doctoral thesis was on hand for the class. She saw how uncomfortable I was in front of all those people. She suggested singing karaoke as a way to get past that fear. She said as silly as it was, by singing in front of all of those people and being reinforced by their applause, it would lessen my fear of public speaking. In the long run, she was right. The first time I went to a bar and sung, I was terrified, but after a couple visits of being positively reinforced, I began to feel more confident. I was able to take that confidence and generalize it to speaking in front of a class. That's why I was thinking it may help you out. Once you realize you can be in the spotlight, sing a song badly, still have people clap for you, and be okay, maybe you'll be able to accept being the nation's hero without the fame weighing so heavily on you."

Tobias grabbed Tracy and kissed her. "Do you know how amazing you are? Who else would not only have noticed I was having an issue with this extra attention but would also have thought of such unique way to help me address it?"

Tracy smiled. "So, what do you think? Are you going to let me take you to a karaoke bar?"

Tobias smiled. "I think it sounds like a fun date night. This will be my first time singing karaoke though, so I am not singing anything alone. We need to do a duet or something."

A large grin appeared on Tracy's face. "I've got the perfect song in mind."

Tobias shook her head. "What song is it?"

Tracy started jogging. "You are just going to have to trust me. I promise it's a song you know and that it's not too hard to sing."

Tobias started jogging after her. "It better not be! If you have me singing some crazy song that I've never heard before, I am going to walk right off the stage!"

When Tobias reached Tracy, he smiled at her. "I will sing whatever duet you want, but you have to sing something for me."

Tracy nodded. "Sure. What song do you want me to sing?"

"Mack the Knife, by Bobby Darin! You know, *When that shark bites. With his teeth dear.* I think given our current situation, it would only be fitting."

Tracy laughed. "You got yourself a deal."

Tracy and Tobias finished their run and then returned to their room. After quick and separate showers, they ate a breakfast of fruit and eggs. Tobias was clearing the table and washing the dishes when the alarm sounded in their room.

Tracy looked over at Tobias. "I guess that means it's go time."

Tobias nodded. "Are you ready to do this or do you need a minute?"

She walked over to Tobias and grabbed his hand. "I feel that I am more ready for this than I have been before." The two of them then walked hand in hand out of their quarters to the neurolink room.

When they entered the neurolink room, Tracy saw Jillian and Mackenzie at their computer stations. Jillian's eyes were fixed on the screen as she prepared the neurolink to sync the pilots with the MEGs.

Mackenzie looked over at them and shouted, "Get into the recliners and sync with the MEGs! They are thirty minutes away from engaging the Mermaid. We will send you information on the target once you are synced with the MEGs."

Tracy and Tobias sprinted over to their recliners. Before putting on her neurolink, Tracy took a quick look at Tobias. He smiled at her and nodded, indicating his complete confidence in their ability to complete the mission. The simple nod and smile helped to increase the young doctor's own confidence that she was ready to sync with MEG 1 and face this new threat.

She smiled back and briefly considered if she and Tobias should have their recliners next to each other so they could be in physical contact with each other when they were synced like Bixby and Munroe were. She put the thought in the back of her mind and made a note to talk to Tobias about it after their mission was complete. Tracy then laid back and pulled her neurolink helmet over her head.

Tracy's vision was momentarily filled with a kaleidoscope of colors and then she saw nothing but black in front of her. It took her a moment to realize it was the middle of the night where MEG 1 was swimming. Tracy calmed her mind and focused on MEG 1's sense of smell and her electroreception abilities. Tracy had experienced the shark's electroreception detection system before, but never in complete darkness. It was an odd feeling to not be able to see anything and yet still be totally aware of everything that was going on around her. To her left, she could sense MEG 2 swimming next to her. Tracy realized that

Tobias was also having the novel experience of knowing where everything around him was despite not being able to see. She made another mental note to discuss this experience as well with Tobias when she had the chance.

MEG 2 swam up next to MEG 1 and Tracy could feel that the monstrous shark was just as comforted by the presence of MEG 2 as she was when Tobias was close by. MEG 2 was close enough to MEG 1 that the shark could roll her eyes toward her male counterpart and see him through the all-enveloping darkness.

Tracy felt a wave of relief rush through her body when she saw MEG 2 looking back at her rather than Tobias. The next thought she had was to remember that MEG 1 was breathing for her underwater so that she did not start drowning the creature again if she panicked.

Tracy could feel the water running through MEG 1's mouth and gills. She had experienced this sensation before, but on prior occasions, she felt as if she was experiencing the sensation as if it was a dream. It was as if she was watching something happen rather than having it happen to her. The young scientist hypothesized that she had achieved a stronger sync with MEG 1 and she wondered if a deeper sync meant she and Tobias had managed to grow in their relationship with each other.

Tracy's thoughts were quickly turned away from her and back to her mission as bright red letters from Mackenzie's computer flashed across her field of vision.

The Mermaid is two hundred and twenty feet long. The monster has a humanoid head, torso, and arms. She has a fish-like lower body with a fluke tail. Her body is covered in thick scales. She has long claws instead of hands and dagger-like teeth. The Mermaid's speed has already been clocked at the upper range of the MEGs' capabilities. However, it is likely that when she enters fight or flight mode, she will be able to swim much faster than our sharks. Our data does confirm that the MEGs outweigh the Mermaid by several thousand tons. In addition to the edge in strength this should give you, the weight difference also suggests that the MEGs are far more durable than the Mermaid. You are fighting in open water, so despite your size, the Mermaid's speed will give her a distinct advantage. You are going to have to coordinate your attacks to kill this monster.

There was a brief flash of light Tracy saw through MEG 1's eyes as Mackenzie's message disappeared. She processed the information and wondered how she was going to be able to coordinate attacks with MEG 2 if she wasn't able to talk to Tobias. Tracy scolded herself for using her time with Tobias to talk about themselves rather than discussing strategy for how to battle the Mermaid and other monsters. As self-doubt crept into her mind, she could feel MEG 1 becoming more restless.

Tracy realized that her connection with MEG 1 had improved to the point that her emotions were affecting the shark. Tracy reminded herself that Tobias was a master strategist and that he would take into account her inexperience. She focused her thoughts on trusting Tobias to enact a plan that would be easy for her to follow and execute even without the benefit of verbal communication. Tracy also reminded herself that she was engaged in a neurolink with a true apex predator. The great white shark was one of the undisputed rulers of the ocean without the benefits of super-size, enhanced abilities, and the mind of a brilliant scientist connected to it. Feelings of confidence and pride flowed through Tracy's mind and into MEG 1, calming the shark down.

Tracy's mind remained calm and focused as the MEGs cruised through the seemingly endless darkness. The colossal cybernetic sharks swam for roughly twenty minutes before their electroreception abilities were able to detect something large swimming in the darkness ahead of them. Tracy could feel that MEG 1 was becoming restless at the possibility of facing an enemy and the prospect of another meal. Tracy urged MEG 1 to continue swimming toward the creature that was stirring in the darkness.

Roughly two miles ahead of the MEGs, the Mermaid was swimming in erratic patterns. The she-creature could sense two large predators entering her territory. In her previous life, the Mermaid was a timid and reclusive creature. She lived a solitary life, only interacting with other members of her species during the breeding season. Most of her life had been spent hunting and avoiding being hunted. When she was smaller before the change, she would have swum to safety at the first indication of a shark moving toward her.

Now, she was a different creature. She was a monster who had been perverted by Rol-Hama. Her mind was filled with the madman's rage and her only thought toward the oncoming predators was to attack and devour them. The Mermaid shifted her bright yellow eyes in the direction of the approaching sharks and started swimming toward them.

The MEGs began to shake their heads from side to side and their heart rates increased as they sensed the Mermaid coming toward them. Tracy and Tobias tried to coordinate the sharks' aggressive tendencies and hunting instincts with their human intelligence. Tracy was looking at the pitch-black water through MEG 1's eyes when she saw two bright yellow orbs swimming toward her. Tracy focused the shark's vision on the seemingly glowing orbs. As the shark looked at the orbs, the oddly humanoid face of the Mermaid started to come into view. Back in her neurolink recliner, Tracy's body shook as she looked at the face of a creature that was utterly monstrous while still possessing an eerily human aspect. For the first time, Tracy was glad that she would primarily be relying on MEG 1's electroreception abilities rather than her vision.

MEG 2 shot past MEG 1 and swam toward the Mermaid. Tracy watched in disbelief as the Mermaid easily dogged MEG 2 by moving to the side and letting the cybernetic shark slide past her. Tracy urged MEG 1 to attack and the shark obeyed by darting toward the Mermaid. MEG 1 had nearly reached the Mermaid when the nimble creature slid out of the way of the shark's attack and gouged the cybernetic creature's side with her claws.

The cut the Mermaid had inflicted was deep and painful. Tracy could feel how much the wound was hurting MEG 1 and she did her best to help the shark focus on the battle rather than on the pain. Tracy saw MEG 2 swim above her as Tobias tried to attack the Mermaid again. MEG 2's jaws were open wide and he was about to bite down on the cryptid when she once more slid just to the side of the attack and then sank her right claw into MEG 2's side. The she-creature then quickly embedded her left claw into the shark's back so that she was attached to the predator. MEG 2 began swimming faster to try and escape from the Mermaid, but the cryptid's claws were sunk too deeply into his body. The Mermaid was still holding onto MEG 2's body when she opened her mouth and sank her vampire-like fangs into the scales at the base of the shark's tail.

Tracy urged MEG 1 to follow her mate and to try and pry the Mermaid free from his body. She watched MEG 2 thrashing violently as he tried to shake the creature off him. MEG 2's efforts to free himself from the tenacious Mermaid were in vain, as the monster refused to release her grip. The Mermaid pulled her left claw out of the shark's back and re-embedded it farther up his side. She then slashed her claw at MEG 2's dorsal fin, only to have one of her fingers sliced off by the diamond-coated steel appendage. The Mermaid shook her claw in pain, causing a cloud of blood to fill the water. MEG 1 swam directly through the cloud as she continued her pursuit of the Mermaid and MEG 2. As the massive shark swam through the cloud of blood, the crimson mist filled her jaws. With her mouth and nostrils filled with blood, the shark's natural instinct to feed was nearly sent into a frenzy.

Back in her neurolink recliner, Tracy squirmed as she struggled to keep the shark's desire to eat from overwhelming her own thoughts.

MEG 1's electroreception sense picked up a massive electrical charge as MEG 2 unleashed his electric attack on the Mermaid. The incredible charge of electricity that was suddenly surging through the Mermaid's body forced her to release her hold on MEG 2.

MEG 2 was free, but he was still bleeding badly as he circled around and prepared to attack the Mermaid again. Tracy could see the Mermaid floating in the water ahead of MEG 1. The monster's body was still shaking from the electrical charge that had wracked her body. Rather than continuing to try and fight MEG 1's feeding instincts, Tracy decided to use them to her advantage. She directed MEG 1 to attack the Mermaid and the ravenous beast obliged the doctor's command. MEG 1 was about to strike the Mermaid when at the last second, Tracy directed the beast to lean to her right. MEG 1 was in the middle of spinning when the Mermaid tried to veer away from her charge. By having MEG 1 lean to her right, Tracy moved the shark away from the Mermaid, but she also had her sharp fin shift toward the creature's body. The end result of Tracy's maneuver was that MEG 1's fin sliced deep into the Mermaid's right tricep and nearly cut her arm in half.

The Mermaid was still writhing in pain as MEG 2 charged her from behind. Mimicking Tracy's attack, Tobias had MEG 2 lean to his left as he approached the she-beast. MEG 2's right fin sliced across the base of the Mermaid's tail as he rocketed past her. More blood began to waft through the water, further inflaming the MEGs' desire to devour the injured cryptid. MEG 1 swam toward the injured Mermaid with the intent of using her fin to further mutilate the monster. The shark rolled as she approached the Mermaid but rather than trying to slide around the attacking shark, the Mermaid moved up and then lifted her tail above her body. As MEG 1 swam beneath her, the Mermaid reached down with her uninjured claw and slashed MEG 1 across her exposed underbelly.

Long red streams of blood streaked out of MEG 1's body and trailed behind her as she moved through the water. In her chair, Tracy grabbed her stomach in response to the pain she was feeling from MEG 1 through the neurolink. Tracy was doing her best to help MEG 1 handle the searing pain in her stomach when she saw MEG 2 streak up past her in pursuit of the Mermaid. Tracy looked up and she saw the fleeing Mermaid making her way toward the surface at a forty-five-degree angle. Despite the pain that she was in, Tracy's brilliant scientific mind suddenly viewed everything around her through a new perspective. She could see the entire ocean like points on a graph with the Mermaid and MEG 2 moving above her along the slope of a triangle.

Tracy combined her knowledge of geometry with one of MEG 1's greatest hunting attacks and she immediately saw how to slay the elusive Mermaid. Tracy directed MEG 1 to swim straight ahead at full speed. By moving straight ahead, while the Mermaid and MEG 2 continued to swim at an angle, Tracy knew MEG 1 would be able to overtake them. Once MEG 1 reached the precise spot that Tracy had calculated she needed to be at, she had the shark swim straight up at a ninety-degree angle.

MEG 1 was streaking toward the surface and with each passing second, more moonlight penetrated the dark ocean and cast a pale glow into the water. The cybernetic shark could see the moon in the sky above the water when the Mermaid suddenly appeared in her line of sight.

In her haste to escape from MEG 2, the Mermaid had forgotten about the larger shark. Tracy could see the monster's yellow eyes filled with terror as she looked down to see MEG 1 charging up toward her. With MEG 1 below her, MEG 2 behind her, and the surface above her, the Mermaid had run out of room to maneuver away from the oncoming attack. The she-creature reached the surface and raised her head into the air at the exact moment that MEG 1 slammed into her from beneath. MEG 1 sank her teeth into the Mermaid's midsection as she breached the water and launched her body into the air.

Through MEG 2's eyes, Tobias watched as the colossal form of MEG 1 shot into the night sky with the moon directly behind her and the Mermaid trapped within her jaws. As the monsters were flying through the air, the Mermaid clawed at MEG 1's body while the shark's teeth sank into her spine. When they crashed back down into water, the Mermaid's spine snapped. Two more powerful bites later, the Mermaid's dead body split into two. MEG 1 grabbed the meaty lower part of the dead cryptid's body and began to devour it while MEG 2 feasted on her torso.

Once Tracy was sure that the Mermaid was dead, she pulled the neurolink helmet off her head. She found herself back in the neurolink room to see Tobias staring at her from his recliner and Mackenzie and Jillian looking at her from their computer stations.

Jillian was the first person to speak. "That was the most amazing thing I have ever seen. I mean, that made air jaws look like a goldfish swallowing a dragonfly on the surface of a pond."

Tobias smiled at his lover. "You were incredible. I've seen pilots with years of experience, with full communication systems up and maps, who can't plot out an attack as well as you just did."

Tracy was still reeling from the emotions she had experienced from MEG 1 as she stared at Tobias. Tracy's eyes were fixed on the pilot when Mackenzie walked over to her and held out his hand to help her out of the recliner. She looked up at the CIA director and for the first time since she had known him, she saw the man smiling. Mackenzie grabbed Tracy's hand and shook his head. "Dr. Curry, I am sorry for ever doubting you. You are an amazing woman, and I have full confidence in your ability to successfully complete this mission."

Tracy nodded at Mackenzie and then she shifted her eyes back to Tobias. Mackenzie helped her out of the chair and he looked briefly at Tobias. "The MEGs will need at least a day of healing their wounds before they are ready to head toward their next target. After that, it will take them about two days to reach the target. That time-frame could shorten if Caddy swims toward the MEGs like the Mermaid and Trunko did." Mackenzie sighed. "Why don't you two plan on taking the next two days off? Don't worry about attending any counseling sessions or briefings. Just take some time to relax; you've earned it."

Tracy ran past Mackenzie and grabbed Tobias' hand. She then led the pilot out of the neurolink room and back toward their quarters. When they left the room, Jillian walked up next to Mackenzie. "Do you think they'll actually get any rest over the next couple of days?"

Mackenzie shrugged. "I don't know. What I do know is when to admit that someone else was right." He turned around and looked at Jillian. "You were right to believe in Tracy." He shrugged. "You were also right when you said that I need to pay more attention to my wife. I am going to take tomorrow off. If anything happens, can you call me?"

Jillian smiled. "Go spend some time with your wife. I'll keep an eye on the world for you tomorrow."

CHAPTER 10
TOKYO BAY AQUA-LINE

Jun Natsuki pulled his car onto the first part of the 24-kilometer-long tunnel-bridge that connected the cities of Kawasaki and Kisarazu. Jun shook his head as he considered how he was going to tell his family that he had been laid off from his job at the shipping firm. He cursed loudly as he thought back about how hard he had worked in school and then in university to land a position at a well-paying company. Jun was respectful to his superiors, and he worked hard days and long nights to move up the corporate chain.

As he moved up the corporate ladder, his life started to fall into place. He was able to marry a fine woman. There was little love in their marriage, but his spouse was a dutiful wife and a good mother. She kept the house and minded the children while he worked and provided for them. Jun's marriage may not have been filled with love, but it was an efficient arrangement. Jun's life plan was to continue to work his way up the chain as his wife raised the children. It was a dream which was going to plan for the middle-aged man up until a few months ago.

Working at a shipping company seemed like a good idea. Japan was an island country and the demand to have supplies shipped into it from various continents would always exist. Jun had worked his way up from an entry-level employee to being responsible for over 25 percent of the company's shipping fleet. For the past several years, Jun had worked at least six days a week and often more than ten hours a day. On a given day, Jun was responsible for making sure that anywhere between thirty and forty ships were able to dock and unload their cargo at various points in the country.

Six months ago, when giant sea monsters started attacking ships all over the world, Jun's work began to slow down. The amount of ships coming into and out of Japan slowed from a raging river to a humble stream. When the giant octopus dubbed Otaka had settled off the coast of Japan, the humble stream of ships going to and from the island country had stopped completely.

When Otaka first appeared, he was attacking ships all over the Pacific Ocean. While the kaiju was extremely aggressive, the sheer size of the ocean made it possible for ships to reach Japan safely. Three months after the attacks had started, Otaka began to make his way toward Japan. Once the kaiju settled off the Japanese coast, the monster virtually shut down the commercial shipping fleet of Japan.

Just as the monster's tentacles put a stranglehold on ships, so did his presence choke the life out of the country itself. Vital supplies such as food, medicine, and gasoline were suddenly cut off from Japan. Without the needed materials from the rest of the world, the island nation was slowly dying.

Food shortages and transportation issues were two of the biggest issues facing the nation, but Jun was worried about losing his job. The fact that he worked at a shipping company was not lost on him. Jun and pretty much everyone else within his company knew that if Otaka was not dealt with, his company would be forced to shut down. To the credit of the managers, they held out as long as they could. The president of the company used his political influence to pressure the government into convincing the Americans to send one of their nuclear submarines to deal with Otaka. Jun can still remember sitting at his desk on the day that the submarine was to engage the kaiju. Like everyone else in his country, he was hoping and praying that the Americans would be able to put an end to the giant cephalopod and return some sense of normality to Japan.

When the news came in that Otaka had crushed the submarine, Jun started preparing for the worst. He liquidated all of his investments and moved them into secure and easily accessible accounts. Despite the fact that he had nothing to do at his job, he still went to work every day. With each passing day, more and more people were being laid off, and Jun could see that the people at the top of the company were working their way up to him.

Today was the day that he had been dreading. Today was the day that his superior called Jun into his office. Jun was told that he had served the company well and that should Otaka be removed and the shipping industry experienced a rebirth, he would be one of the first people to have his position restored. Jun bowed and thanked his superior. He then walked out of the office and started to drive home.

Jun shook his head again as he looked over the side of the bridge at the bay. Jun felt like he had lost more than just a job. He felt as if he had lost his purpose in life, his very soul. Jun's job was everything to him. His career was what defined him and gave his life meaning. Without it, he was nothing.

Jun was still staring at the bay when he saw a large bulbous form suddenly appear out of the water. It looked as if a mound made of pure mucus had risen out of the bay and was moving toward the Aqua-Line.

Jun rolled down his window to get a better look at the strange mound and when he did so, a horrible stench blew in from off the river.

Jun's faced winced as he gagged from the rancid stench. Once he had managed to swallow the bile that had come up into his mouth, he looked back out at the bay to see huge tentacles rising out of the water and splashing back down into the bay. At the sight of the tentacles, a wave of terror ran through Jun's body. Jun whispered to himself. "Otaka has entered Tokyo Bay."

Jun was in disbelief at the fact that the monster was in the bay until the car to the left of him swerved into his lane and hit his passenger-side door. Jun's car was shifted to the right. As he was pushed closer to the edge of the Aqua-Line, he quickly looked over to see Otaka's dark black soulless eyes peering out of the water and staring at the bridge. When Jun saw Otaka's eyes, he knew the monster that had taken his job had now come to take his life.

Jun pressed his accelerator to the floor and started speeding ahead. He was swerving in and out of cars that were slowing down or coming to a complete stop to look at the giant octopus as it made its way toward the bridge. After seeing the reports of what Otaka had done to the merchant ships and the U.S. submarine, he knew the monster would crush the bridge section of the Aqua-Line to pieces.

Jun cursed when he saw a wall of parked cars in front of him. It appeared as if he had not been the only one to see the monster coming toward the Aqua-Line. Rows of cars had come to a stop in front of a huge pile-up of vehicles which had crashed at the site of the monster. Jun pulled his car to stop and stepped out to see other people walking over to the side of the bridge to look at the oncoming kaiju. Jun walked over to join them and he breathed a small sigh of relief when he saw that Otaka was still moving in a straight line. Jun was fairly sure he had moved beyond the reach of the kaiju's tentacles. He didn't know the exact size of Otaka, but Jun figured that he had put at least half a kilometer between himself and where the monster would reach the bridge. He looked back down the bridge to see more cars coming to a stop. With each car that came to a stop, panicked people jumped out of their vehicles and started running out of the direct path of the oncoming cephalopod.

Otaka had nearly reached the bridge when a huge explosion rocked the bridge behind Jun. The force of the blast knocked the former businessman and everyone around him to the ground. Jun felt a sharp pain on his back and head. He was disoriented and his ears were ringing. The man next to him was moving his mouth like he was shouting, but all

Jun could hear was the loud ringing sound reverberating in his ears. Jun stood up and looked behind him to see that several of the cars in the middle of the pileup had exploded. There was now a massive fire raging in the middle of the bridge, blocking traffic in both directions.

The shouting man grabbed Jun and turned him around to face the water. Once Jun was turned around, he saw why the man was shouting. The explosion had caught Otaka's attention. The kaiju was now heading directly for the section of the bridge that he was standing on. Jun turned back around to run from the oncoming monster only to be faced with the wall of fire from the burning cars behind him. Jun spun back the other way to see Otaka's tentacles slithering up the sides of the bridge.

The people who had gathered near the edge of the bridge slowly began to back away from the encroaching tentacles. The people who were nearest to the edge of the bridge started to push up against those behind them. The people they ran into had little room to move with the inferno burning behind them. Jun was slowly starting to be pushed back by the crowd when one of Otaka's tentacles rose high into the air. In unison, everyone standing on the bridge shifted their heads skyward toward the towering appendage.

The aquatic kaiju brought his tentacle crashing down onto the bridge. The impact of the blow crushed the people it struck to a pulp and smashed the section of the bridge it hit into the bay. Jun was once more knocked to the ground as the collapsing bridge shook beneath him. He looked up to see more of Otaka's tentacles rising up above the bridge and then he saw the kaiju's hideous face peering down at the hundreds of people trapped below him. Jun heard a woman scream and then the crowd of people trapped between the monster and the inferno panicked.

Jun was starting to stand when he was suddenly trampled back to the ground by the panicked mob as they tried to escape the monster's wrath. Jun felt his bones being broken as people stepped on him. He knew that he was going to die if he stayed on the ground. Through the stampede of people stepping on him, Jun saw a large cargo truck a few feet to his left. Jun started rolling to his left, causing more people to trip and fall. Jun rolled over one of the people he had knocked down. With one final roll, Jun's body slid under the truck.

Jun's face was bloody, bruised, and swollen, but he was able to see what was going on around him. The first thing that he saw was the man he had tripped when he was rolling and being trampled by the crowd of people. The man wasn't moving and Jun was fairly sure he was dead. Jun was contemplating his role in the man's demise when one of Otaka's tentacles came crashing down and crushed everyone in his view.

The bridge once more shook with the impact. When the tentacle lifted back into the air, Jun saw a smear of blood, bones, clothes, and skin where the tentacle had landed. There was another impact, and Jun felt the bridge starting to give way beneath him. It was at that moment that Jun's life flashed before his eyes. He saw a collage of his days at school and various business meetings. What he did not see were his wife and kids.

Jun felt a flood of shame and disappointment in himself at the way he had neglected his family. To his surprise, the bridge briefly stopped shaking. Realizing that the bridge was somehow still partially intact, Jun quickly formed a plan to try and escape the looming death he was facing. Jun rolled out from the under the truck to see Otaka wrapping his tentacles around the bridge. The reinvigorated father knew he only had one chance of escaping the bridge before the kaiju tore it down and sent it tumbling into the bay.

Jun ran over to the carnage Otaka had left in his wake when he crushed the people next to the truck. Jun grabbed as many blood-soaked clothes as he could and he wrapped them around his body. As Jun wrapped a bloody sports coat around his head, he could feel pieces of organs pressing against his face. Jun had covered the majority of his body when he felt the bridge shaking beneath him. He covered his eyes as best as he could and then he ran toward the car fire. With his vision obscured by smoke, Jun ran into car side-view mirrors and open doors. Jun could feel the heat growing in intensity as he pushed nearer to the fire. Jun was terrified that he would be burned to death by the inferno, but he also knew that if he stayed where he was, he would be crushed to death when the bridge gave way. The thought of seeing his family one more time gave Jun the courage to move forward. He jumped into the flames, hoping that the clothes and blood of the people who had already died would be enough to grant him one more chance at life.

Jun was in the flames for matter of seconds, but in that timeframe, the heat from the fire burned him badly. Jun released a scream of mixed pain, fear, and determination as he pushed through the blaze. Jun was nearly through the flames when he tripped and fell. He hit the ground hard and then forced his burned and blistered body to roll as far as it could. He rolled until he hit something and then he and stopped. He heard the terrible sound of steel, concrete, and metal being crushed and falling into the bay. He used his scorched fingers to peel the sports coat from around his head and saw the section of the bridge Otaka had within his grasp falling into the bay.

Jun saw the massive octopus, tons of debris, cars, bodies, and still-living people falling into the bay below. For a brief moment, everything was still and then several of Otaka's tentacles rose back into the air. Jun stood up and he began limping along the bridge, heading for a tunnel he saw in the distance. As he limped along, Jun could hear more sections of the bridge being torn down. Jun knew that with each crashing sound, hundreds of people were dying. The only comfort in the sound was that it seemed to be moving away from Jun's direction. Whether through divine intervention or sheer luck, Otaka seemed to be destroying the bridge and moving along in the opposite direction from the way Jun was walking.

Jun kept staring forward as he moved along. He could hear the devastation taking place behind him, but he could not bring himself to turn around and look it. Behind Jun, countless people were dying. Those people would never make it home to hug their kids again or kiss their spouses. Jun began to tear up as he made a silent promise to the dying that he would use what remained of his life to no longer take his loved ones for granted.

Jun limped along for thirty minutes until he reached the tunnel. When he reached the tunnel, he saw a crowd of people staring in silence at the scene of horror taking place further down the bridge. Jun didn't turn around; he just kept staring at the tunnel. He saw a woman holding a cell phone in her hand. He asked the woman if he could use the phone and she slowly handed it over to him. Jun dialed his home number and despite the terrible pain he was in, he smiled when his eldest son answered the phone.

CHAPTER 11

Tracy and Tobias walked into their appointment with Dr. Vaughn. It had been two days since their last mission and the two young lovers were well-rested and had some time to process their battles with both Trunko and the Mermaid. The two of them walked into the office and sat down. Tracy was still annoyed by having to attend the session. She felt that she and Tobias were growing closer to each other as evidenced by their performance in their last mission. She had mentioned as much to Tobias, and he said that while he understood her feelings, he was still ordered to attend the session and as a member of the U.S. Air Force, he was obligated to follow his orders.

Tracy was glad that Tobias had acknowledged her concerns, but she was still disappointed that their personal relationship was under the purview of the U.S. government. When they entered the office, Tracy briefly acknowledged Dr. Vaughn and then she sat down on the couch facing the doctor's chair. She was surprised when Tobias did not immediately sit down next to her but rather stood in front of Dr. Vaughn. Tracy could see that Tobias wanted to say something to the counselor, but he was having difficulty finding the words to express his thoughts.

Tobias was still standing in front of Vaughn when the doctor addressed him. "Tobias, is there something that you would like to say to me?"

Tobias cleared his throat. "Yes, ma'am. Forgive me. This is the first time I have ever had to do something like this and it's difficult for me. I am a member of the U.S. Air Force, and I am attending this session under direct orders. As I am obligated to carry out those orders, I will follow them to the best of my ability and stay here for the duration of the session." He looked over toward Tracy. "Dr. Curry, however, is a civilian contractor, and she is under no obligation to follow orders given by superior officers. I would respectfully request that Dr. Curry be allowed to cease attending these sessions immediately. I believe that our relationship is progressing at an acceptable rate as evidenced by our last mission. As per procedure, I have made a formal written request to Director Mackenzie as well, citing our last mission as evidence of our progress."

Tracy stood up as her mind and heart were flooded with pride and love toward Tobias. She knew how difficult it was for him to do anything that was against the orders of a superior officer and yet here he was doing just that, for her benefit.

Dr. Vaughn saw Tracy standing there and she remained purposefully silent as the young doctor walked over to the pilot. Tracy wrapped her arms around her boyfriend. "Tobias, you could have told me back in our quarters you were going to do this. Why did you have me walk all the way down here with you?"

Tobias looked down at the floor. "For two reasons. The first is that I needed you here to draw strength from because I knew going against a superior officer's orders was going to be difficult for me. The second reason is, I wanted you to see me do it. I wanted you to see that I was willing to do something that I never thought I could do for you."

Tracy lifted Tobias' head so that his eyes were looking into hers. "I love you." She kissed him and then turned to Dr. Vaughn. "I think our relationship is progressing just fine. I won't make Tobias stay here alone." She smiled. "Besides, he'd probably only respond to yes and no questions anyway." Tobias smiled and nodded in reply. Tracy grabbed Dr. Vaughn by the hand. "Would it be okay if for the next couple of sessions we talked about what it's like syncing with the MEGs? I know Tobias has shared his mind with a cybernetic monster before, but for me, this is a new experience and I could really use a venue where I can discuss how this is affecting me."

Dr. Vaughn smiled. "Given your last mission and what I have seen here today, I think we can put your couples therapy sessions on hold for a while." She grabbed Tobias' hand. "You need not worry, Captain Crow. I will also make an official recommendation to Director Mackenzie that your couples therapy sessions end. I will, however, add onto my report the recommendation for additional psychological counseling to deal with your experiences of syncing with the MEGs if the two of you so wish?"

Tracy nodded. "Let's see how this session goes and we can go from there." She turned to Tobias. "If that's good for you?"

Tobias shrugged. "Like you said, let's see how this session goes."

The two lovers walked back toward the couch and Dr. Vaughn sat down in her chair. Before Vaughn could even ask her first question, Tracy started talking about the battle with the Mermaid. " I think that I have finally found a balance with MEG 1. When we were fighting the Mermaid, it was the first time I was not only able to feel what MEG 1 was feeling but also understand her perspective on it." Tracy smiled as her body shook with excitement. "When I saw how MEG 2 was chasing the Mermaid, somehow the way I viewed the ocean as a graph and MEG 1 saw it as her hunting grounds just all came together. Usually, I feel like I am doing my best to coordinate my efforts with MEG 1, but at that moment, it seemed like we were on the same page. Like our minds were truly one and we were taking the best parts of both our thought processes to address the problem." Tracy stood up. "I felt like MEG 1 and I were slowly making progress toward this, but I always felt like there was some kind of invisible barrier that we both had to overcome from opposite sides. When we managed to break through that barrier, it was as if we shared one goal, one mind, one heart. It was like by opening ourselves up to each other and seeing things from the other's perspective, we were able to get the best out of each other."

Tracy's eyes suddenly grew wide as she turned around and looked at Tobias. "It's just like me and Tobias." She sat down next to him and grabbed his hand as she continued talking to Dr. Vaughn. "When Tobias and I were on the same page, when we finally understood each other, when we saw things from the other's perspective, that's when we were able to function at peak efficiency. By really understanding each other, we were able to optimize each other's strengths and compensate for our weaknesses." Tracy looked over at Tobias. "My God, I developed the neurolink. How could I not see this from the start?"

Dr. Vaughn grabbed her hand. "My dear, a relationship is a journey. You must learn as you progress through it. It is entirely possible that were it not for your connection with MEG 1 and your relationship with Tobias that you may not have fully understood what it meant to sync with another being."

Tracy's face changed as the scientist in her began to form a new hypothesis. "I wonder if strengthening my relationship with Tobias helped me to better sync with MEG 1, did forming a deeper sync with MEG 1 help me to strengthen my relationship with Tobias?"

Vaughn shrugged. "Perhaps it did. Maybe that is something you should research if you go forward with your neurolink project." Tracy nodded in reply as her mind came to terms with the progress she had made. Vaughn turned her head toward Tobias. "What about you Captain Crow? How have your recent experiences with MEG 2 differed from those in the past, as well as the times that you were synced with ROC 1?"

Tobias shrugged. "I think it's similar to what Tracy was saying. I don't have a single moment I can point to like Tracy, but I feel that MEG 2 and I have a better understanding of each other than ROC 1 and I did." He sighed. "Or at least I have a better understanding of MEG 2 than I did of ROC 1." He looked toward Tracy. " I mean this in a good way, but being with Tracy had made me uncomfortable in a lot of ways. Being with her has made me do things that I would have shied away from in the past. Things like expressing my feelings to other people or bucking the orders of a commanding officer." He shrugged as he looked at Tracy. "I know what you mean about a wall. For all of the danger I have faced in my life, I have always kept a wall around myself to prevent me from getting hurt by people who are close to me or to prevent me from hurting them. It was the same wall that kept me from letting ROC 1 into my head. The same wall that cost ROC 1 his life. It was because I tried to force what I thought was the best of me on ROC 1 rather than finding what was the best of the two of us that he died." He squeezed Tracy's hand a little harder. "When I am out there with you, I want to make sure you make it home safe. You mean more to me than anything. The desire to see you again and the way in which you have helped me to face my fears and feelings has torn down that wall. I also feel that MEG 2 and I are getting the best of out of each other. I feel like we can destroy any monster we come across. Thanks to you." Tobias leaned over and kissed Tracy.

Dr. Vaughn smiled. "I think you two have had enough counseling for one day. The best thing you can do at this point is to go and enjoy the day. As I understand it, you have roughly twenty-four hours until the MEGs are ready to engage their next target?"

Tobias broke away from Tracy and nodded. "Yes, ma'am."

Vaughn stood up. "Then I suggest you two continue to foster the beautiful relationship you are forming. Then take what you have learned from the growth you have made and apply it to killing some sea monsters." Tracy and Tobias laughed and then they left the office hand in hand.

CHAPTER 12
SEAWORLD, MISSION BAY PARK, SAN DIEGO

It was a beautiful and sunny day at the world's largest aquatic-themed amusement park. Despite the fact that the worldwide economy was slowly sinking into a deep depression, SeaWorld was still managing to turn a profit. When they saw that most of the ocean-based tourist attractions around the world were shut down due to the threat of sea monsters attacking, they quickly lowered their prices. The theme park's administrators were fully aware that a large portion of the population had a deeply ingrained desire to interact with the ocean. They also knew that if the people who had this urge were unable to fulfill that desire on the open ocean or on beaches, they would look for another outlet.

SeaWorld San Diego was built in part of the largest man-made bay in North America. The park provided people with the opportunity to see animal attractions that could only be seen in the wild by the most ardent adventurers. Before the world was threatened by giant monster attacks, SeaWorld San Diego presented a unique experience for tourists. In the current situation, their park full of rides, shows, and location on a protected in land bay served as the only way people could access the pleasures of the ocean and escape the harsh reality of the threats they were facing.

When worldwide shipping shut down, SeaWorld dropped its ticket prices by over fifty percent. As a result of the ticket price drop, their attendance increased by nearly five times their normal rate. People were sick of the reality of giant monsters. SeaWorld and Mission Bay provided people with a way to forget about that reality for a while.

The main attraction at the park was their world famous Orca Encounter attraction. With the park at full capacity and Shamu Stadium filled past the point of standing room only, the handlers had all seven of their orcas on display. The majestic animals were throwing themselves into the air and crashing back down into the water to the delight of a crowd that was longing for a break from the stress of their fears.

In the water outside of Mission Bay, Caddy was cruising up and down the California coast. Prior to his increase in size due to exposure from the Branson formula, the creature ate mainly fish and small mammals. Now that he was more than five times his previous size, Caddy had found he required whales, orcas, dolphins, and large sharks to sustain him. At first, the monster had found hunting relatively easy as the prey he sought were accustomed to sitting at the top of the food chain. After a few weeks of hunting, however, the prey the monster sought had become aware of his presence and fled the area. As a result of this mass exodus, Caddy was forced to search for new waters in which he could hunt.

As the monster swam past the entrance to Mission Bay, he caught the scent of not only the orcas and other sea life at SeaWorld but also of the throngs of people gathered there. Caddy swam back and forth across the opening to the man-made bay. The monster somehow realized that Mission Bay was not a natural formation and for a few moments, that thought kept him from entering the estuary. After swimming back and forth for nearly an hour, the scent of the sea life and the people in the park drove the hungry monster into a frenzy. Caddy's horse-like head rose out of the water as his serpentine neck extended into the sky. The cryptid looked in the direction of SeaWorld and unleashed a terrifying roar. The monster then dove back into the water and entered the bay.

David Caffery was the head of security at SeaWorld San Diego. He was sitting in his office watching the video feeds of the thousands of people who were enjoying the park and whose safety was his responsibility. David had just unpacked his lunch, and was looking forward to his first break of what had already been a very busy day, when his phone rang.

David groaned as he answered the phone. "Hello, this David Caffery, head of SeaWorld security."

The voice on the other end of the phone was hurried. "Mr. Caffery, this is Donna Washington with the U.S. Coast Guard. We are tracking the sea monster known as Caddy. He has recently entered Mission Bay and he appears to be headed toward SeaWorld!"

David knocked his lunch to the floor as he shot up from his chair. "What! You people told us Caddy wouldn't enter the bay!" David took a deep breath. "It's alright. Just in case something like this happens, we have severely limited any activities on the open water. The only bay activity that is open is the fenced-off wading pool. I'll call everyone in from it right away."

Donna Washington's voice took on an even graver tone. "No, Mr. Caffery! You don't understand the full gravity of this situation! Caddy has shown the ability to maneuver on land for short periods of time!"

David dropped the phone from his hand and grabbed the park-wide microphone. "This is the head of SeaWorld security! We need all guests and staff to exit the park in an orderly fashion and to proceed to the parking lot. Repeat, this is the head of SeaWorld security. We need all guests and staff to exit the park in an orderly fashion and to proceed to the parking lot!"

He took one look at his security cameras to see SeaWorld staff calmly directing people out of whatever attraction they were at. He was glad to see that all of the hours of training he had run the staff through in the event of evacuation was paying off. The staff was moving guests out of the park and no one was panicking. David turned away from his cameras and he walked outside of the security center to a pavilion that was overlooking the bay. When he saw a massive creature rise out of the water less than hundred meters from where he was standing, he knew that the park would never be evacuated in time. With Caddy bearing down upon him, David pulled out his phone and called his wife. When she answered the phone, he calmly said. "Honey, I just wanted to say that I love you and tell you how happy you have made me." As soon as he finished his sentence, a wave of water slammed into him and knocked him to the ground. He was just starting to stand when Caddy's body slithered over him and crushed him to death.

Caddy lifted his head high into the air and sniffed the vast array of aromas wafting from the various displays and tanks. The sea serpent began to drool as the scent of food increased the hunger pains he was feeling. Caddy dropped onto his stomach, crushing the former security center to the ground. Then like a massive snake, he began slithering toward Shamu Stadium.

As people were calmly exiting the orca exhibit, the killer whales began to frantically swim back and forth in their tank. In what sounded like a cacophony of sorrow, the orcas began letting out frantic high-pitched calls. One of the majestic creatures swam to the bottom of the tank and then rocketed to the water's surface, throwing her body into the air.

Two of the trainers who were directing people out of the stadium were watching the strange behaviors of the whales. One of them turned to the other. "They are really acting up. Maybe an earthquake is coming."

The other trainer took a look back at the tank and screamed when she saw the horrifying form of Caddy rising up from behind the stadium. The sea serpent roared and then dove into the orca tank. The enlarged cryptid's body was so colossal that it filled up nearly the entire tank. When Caddy entered the tank, a wall of water rose over the edge of its wall and slammed into the first five rows of seats in the stadium, causing people to tumble down the concrete stairs and metal bleachers.

Caddy righted his body in the tank as the orcas swam over and around him. He saw one of the whales swimming in front of his face and he closed his jaws on the creature, biting her in half. As Caddy devoured the front half of his first victim, the other whales began slamming into the sides of their tank in a desperate attempt to escape the looming death that had entered their enclosure.

The stadium was only partially evacuated and the people were still in the stands when Caddy attacked. The people who were still in top rows of seats gave up on trying to make their way down the stairs and they began climbing over the soaked and slippery bleachers in an attempt to escape the horror that was taking place before them. As people were forcing their way down the stairs, they pushed others out of the way or knocked them to the ground.

Caddy devoured the orca that was in his mouth then he quickly twisted around and went for another of the terrified whales. Caddy opened his mouth wide and then snapped his jaws shut just behind the orca as the mammal swam away from the monster. Caddy hissed, shifted his head, and continued his pursuit of his next victim. The whale that Caddy was chasing swam to the side of the tank and then, with nowhere left to go, the orca swam straight up. When the orca reached the surface of the water, he threw his body over the edge of the tank and toward the stands. The people who were still trying to exit the stadium caught a brief glimpse of the orca over their heads before the beast fell on top of them and crushed them. Those closest to the floundering whale only had the briefest moment to scream before Caddy sank his teeth into the orca and lifted it into the air. The sea serpent swallowed the whale in two bites then he looked down at the mass of humans below him. Caddy hissed again then his head shot down toward the mob of fleeing humans. The cryptid scooped up a mouthful of humans and swallowed them whole. The cryptid continued to eat the people trapped in the stadium until every last human was devoured.

Caddy's long body was draped over the blood-soaked bleachers of Shamu Stadium when he looked back at the five orcas still trapped in their tank. Caddy hissed and then he slithered back toward his original prey. The serpent devoured two more whales before deciding he had his fill. The creature then curled his body around the bottom of the tank as the remaining three orcas continued to crash into the sides of tank in a vain attempt to flee for their lives. The monster knew that he had a viable food source in the park that would last him for several days. Aside from the three orcas swimming above him, Caddy could smell dolphins, sea turtles, large rays, polar bears, and whales all trapped within the park.

The monster closed his eyes, satisfied that he had found his new hunting grounds.

BALTIMORE

George Mackenzie rushed into Jillian Creen's office. She was sitting at her computer and reviewing the information from Caddy's attack in SeaWorld. Jillian turned toward Mackenzie. "I'm sorry you only got to spend one day with your family."

Mackenzie shrugged. "The important part is that I made it a good day." The CIA director quickly refocused the conversation on the current crisis. "What's going on with the attack in California, and why are the sea monsters in general attacking sites closer to shore or in some cases on shore?"

Jillian sighed. "I am going to answer your questions in reverse order. First, we think that Rol-Hama's command to the sea monsters may have included some kind of impulse to attack shorelines if worldwide shipping came to a stop. This directive may also be tied into the monster's hunting instincts. As of right now, we are not quite sure. Caddy is stationary at the bottom of a tank in SeaWorld. We think he is going to stay in the park until he eats all of the animals trapped there. The MEGs can't get to him there. What do we do? Bomb SeaWorld while Caddy is sleeping in the orca tank?"

Mackenzie shook his head. "No. Short of a nuke, that monster would survive any conventional weapon we could throw at it. The way to get this monster is by pooling our resources. The MEGs still have twelve hours of swimming ahead of them before they reach Mission Bay. If the ROCs fly at top speed from Africa, they can reach Mission Bay in that same time period."

Jillian's face became slightly concerned. "If we do have the ROCs attack a monster on the U.S. West Coast, we will leave the entire Indian Ocean open to attack from the Shojo. He's the one creature who poses a potential extended land-based threat. We could be leaving a major port city open to attack in order to kill a monster who is currently stationed in a theme park and as far as we know can only be out of the water for short periods of time. Are you sure that taking out Caddy is worth the risk of a Shojo attack on a large city?"

Mackenzie clenched his fists. "It's a tough call, but Caddy is on U.S. soil and we have a unique opportunity to take him out. Caddy is a clear and imminent threat. We are going to put an end to that threat while we have the chance."

Jillian shook her head. "What about moving one of the ROCs to Mission Bay and leaving the other in Africa?"

Mackenzie threw his hands into the air. "We know that the ROCs are most effective in tandem. If we split them up, we drastically increase our chances of losing both of them. I'll take the odds of two ROCs and two MEGs vs one sea serpent over one ROC taking on the aquatic version of Bigfoot. Have Munroe and Bixby get the ROCs into the air. They are going to attack Caddy while he is in SeaWorld. As you stated, Caddy can only maneuver on land for a short period of time and he is not particularly adept at doing it. The ROCs' objective will be to either destroy Caddy or at the very least to drive him into the bay where the MEGs will be waiting for him!" He turned away from Jillian. "If the Shojo makes a move on a land-based target, it will be on my head."

CHAPTER 13
BALTIMORE

Tracy Curry and Tobias Crow walked into the debriefing room to find Mackenzie and Jillian there staring at a computer screen with Lindsay Munroe's and David Bixby's faces on it. When the two ROC pilots saw their former team leader walk into the room, their faces let up. Munroe smiled. "Crow, how have you been? Are you used to being synced with a monster that moves through the ocean like a bubble head yet instead of soaring through the sky?"

Crow shrugged. "It's pretty much the same thing. It's just a little harder to maneuver in the water than it was in the air."

Tracy walked up to the screen. "Hey guys, I know it's only been a few months since we last saw you, but it feels like forever. How is everything going for you two?"

Bixby blushed as Munroe held out her hand to show a diamond ring. Tracy and Jillian both screamed with joy. Munroe smiled. "Yes, he finally proposed to me. You know, you kill a half-dozen giant monsters together and figure from there, marriage is the only logical next step."

Jillian smiled. "How did you do it, David?"

Bixby shrugged. "Well, after she told me that it was about damn time I proposed to her, I went out and bought a ring."

Before Bixby could tell any more of the story, Mackenzie cut him off. "Congratulations to you both, but we can talk about wedding plans later. Right now, we have to discuss how the ROCs and MEGs are going to work together to attack Caddy." Mackenzie looked at his watch. "The MEGs will be entering Mission Bay in about half an hour and the ROCs will reach SeaWorld forty-five minutes after that." Mackenzie brought up an image of Caddy on the screen, along with all of the vital information on the monster.

Bixby moved his face closer to the screen. "That monster looks an awful lot like Nessie, doesn't he?"

Mackenzie nodded. "Yes, Caddy has the same serpentine features with small appendages that allow it to move on land that Nessie possessed. Our data shows that Caddy is smaller and lighter than Nessie. Obviously, we are not cryptozoologists, but it's possible that Caddy and Nessie are members of the same or similar species."

Munroe pushed her fiancé aside to get a better look at the monster they would be facing. "Right now, this monster is sitting in the bottom of a tank, right?" Mackenzie nodded his head in affirmation of the young pilot's question. Munroe smiled. "Then the attack plan is easy. We have the ROC 2 and ROC 4 fly over the tank spraying their liquid nitrogen. If we are lucky, we freeze Caddy solid in the tank. If he gets out, we use the same distract and attack method we used on Nessie. One ROC flies toward the monster's face and then pulls back while the other one hits him from behind. Either way, this monster is taken out quickly and we can get back to the Indian Ocean and look for that overgrown sea monkey."

Mackenzie nodded. "I think that's the best plan of attack. The only difference between this mission and when the ROCs took out Nessie is that the bay is less than one hundred meters from Caddy's current position. The monster can move quickly on land in short bursts. If he makes it to the water, we will have the MEGs there to address the threat." Mackenzie turned toward Tracy and Tobias. "If you have to engage Caddy in the bay, it will be different from your battles in the open ocean. The bay is a far shallower setting than you have fought monsters in so far. You won't be able to use depth to your advantage like you did against the Mermaid. The bay will force you into a head-on battle with Caddy. It could get very bloody really quickly."

Tobias reached over and grabbed Tracy's hand. She squeezed it and then looked sternly into Mackenzie's eyes. "We can handle it if it comes to that."

Mackenzie nodded. "All right then, that's our plan. The ROCs take the first shot at Caddy. If he makes it to the water, the MEGs will engage him while the ROCs fly over the bay looking to provide any support they can. Do we all understand the plan?"

A resounding, "Yes, sir!" came from all four pilots.

Mackenzie nodded. "Good. Curry, Crow, I want you two synced with MEGs and I want them to swim around the bay as much as possible prior to the ROCs engaging Caddy. I want you two to be aware of every dip and shallow point in the bay. Knowledge of the terrain could win or lose this fight." Tracy and Tobias both nodded. Mackenzie turned around. "Okay, let's get this mission underway."

Mackenzie was leaving the room when Tracy slowly walked closer to the computer screen and called out to Bixby and Munroe. "Guys, I know that we have never been particularly close, but when this is all over, can Tobias and I talk to you two a little bit? You are the only other two people in the world who have had to build a relationship with each other while trying to sync with a giant monster. I feel like you two are the only people who can relate to what Tobias and I are going through and we could really use someone who can empathize with us to talk to."

Munroe smiled. "Sure, Dr. Curry, but don't be surprised if you and I do most of the talking while David and Crow just sit there quietly. You know them and that whole strong, silent type can't talk about their feelings thing."

Bixby shook his head. "Hey, being able to talk to you about my feelings for you saved the world, remember?"

Munroe punched her fiancé in the arm. "Yeah, it took the world being on the line for you to realize that you had feelings for me."

Bixby shrugged. "Well, that's the same story for you."

Tracy smiled at the familiar banter between the two. "Thanks, guys, I now have no doubts that you two are the people we need to talk to. Right now, we better get moving or Mackenzie it going to lose it." Everyone said their goodbyes and then the screen went blank. Tracy walked over toward Tobias who smiled. "If those two hotheads can make things work enough to save the world, it should be a walk in the park for us."

Tracy smiled. "You read my mind." She then grabbed his hand and together they walked to the neurolink station. As they were walking down the hallway, Tracy looked over at Tobias. "As our missions progress and we get to know each other better, I am learning the value of being able to anticipate your teammates' moves. You and I are getting better at knowing how we use our MEGs in the field, but how will we communicate with Bixby and Munroe during the mission?"

Tobias shrugged. "I've worked with them long enough to have a pretty good idea of what they are going to do. Even if I hadn't been a part of the ROC program, they are experienced enough to know how to work around someone who is new in the field."

Tracy nodded. "I guess it's like when I have to work with a grad student on a project and I have to anticipate where they could screw up. It's just been a while since I was the grad student and potential screw up."

Tobias stopped walking, placed his hand on Tracy's chin, and turned her head so they were looking into each other's eyes. "Don't doubt yourself. Being self-confident is one way to strengthen your sync with MEG 1. You also have every reason to be confident. It was you who really took the lead in the last mission and enacted the plan that killed the Mermaid. Even if I wasn't in love with you, I would still say you have made more progress in syncing with MEG 1 than any of the ROC pilots made in such a short amount time."

Tracy smiled. "Thanks, Tobias." The two them entered the neurolink room to see Mackenzie and Jillian at their computer consoles, ready for mission launch. Tracy walked Tobias over to his recliner, kissed him, and then watched as he sat down and slid on his neurolink helmet. She then walked over to her recliner, climbed into it, and pulled her neurolink helmet on. Tracy saw the usual flash of light and then she saw brightly lit water all around here. MEG 1 was swimming in shallow water near the entrance to Mission Bay. Tracy was used to piloting the monster cyborg as she left Chesapeake Bay, but this was different. The water around the giant shark was already nearly as shallow as the Chesapeake was at low tide. Tracy took a deep breath as she realized how shallow the man-made bay truly was.

MEG 2 swam up next to MEG 1 and briefly brushed against her. Typically, this behavior would not be taken well by the shark who was brushed up against. In this instance, however, MEG 1 was synced well enough with Tracy to know that MEG 2's contact was a gesture from Tobias to help soothe her nerves. As a result, rather than acting aggressively, MEG 1 also felt comforted by the act. The gesture of support from Tobias and the realization of how strong her sync with MEG 1 had become gave Tracy a sense of calm confidence. Tracy was able to convey that feeling to MEG 1 and as Tracy directed the cybernetic monster into the entrance of Mission Bay, the young neuroscientist felt as if she could conquer all of the remaining sea monsters she had to face at once.

Tracy's heightened sense of confidence was exactly what MEG 1 needed. The bay was so shallow that the colossal shark barely fit in it. Even with her dorsal fin and the tip of her tail sticking out of the water, MEG 1 only had one hundred and twenty feet of space between her stomach and the bottom of the bay. MEG 2 slid past MEG 1 on her left and started traversing the bay.

Through MEG 2, Tobias took Tracy on a quick trip around the bay. When they came across a particularly shallow area of the bay, MEG 2 would shift his head toward it so that Tracy was aware of it. The head shift was followed up by a message flashing across her vision from Mackenzie's computer indicating the same thing.

Be careful around this area. Don't get the MEGs beached when trying to fight or avoid Caddy. Stats forthcoming. Caddy is a two hundred and eighty foot long sea serpent. He will use his body in the same manner as a constrictor snake by wrapping it around an enemy and crushing him. In addition to his ability to crush his prey, Caddy also has long, dagger-like teeth.

As MEG 2 led Tracy and MEG 1 back toward the entrance of the bay, MEG 1's eyes noticed a huge shadow passing over her. The shark's dark black eyes rotated upward to see the awesome forms of ROC 2 and ROC 4 flying overhead. The cybernetic birds circled over the bay to make sure they had the MEGs' attention. When MEG 2 noticed the ROCs circling above him, Tobias directed his shark to start swimming back toward SeaWorld. Tracy directed MEG 1 to follow him and then she readied her mind for battle.

The ROCs did one slow flyover of SeaWorld in order to see the layout of the park, as well as to identify their prey. Finding Caddy was a relatively easy task. The sea serpent was still lying at the bottom of the orca tank. The tank itself was red from the blood of its former inhabitants while pieces of the slain orcas floated on the water's surface. What remained of Shamu Stadium was littered with the chewed-up and severed body parts of the humans who had been trapped there during Caddy's attack.

The two ROCs landed on either side of the decimated stadium and then they slowly approached the gore-filled tank. ROC 2 and ROC 4 briefly looked at each other then they bent over and opened their beaks. A bright white mist started to emanate from the ROCs' beaks. The moment that the liquid nitrogen spray hit the water, it began to turn it into ice.

At the bottom of the quickly freezing tank, Caddy's eyes snapped open as the monster was awakened by the dramatic drop in temperature. Caddy roared and then started swimming toward the surface. When he was close to the surface, Caddy's head slammed into a thick sheet of ice. The monster roared in frustration and then swung his tail around, shattering the wall of ice that was preventing him from escaping the freezing water.

Caddy popped his head up through the hole in the ice and he was immediately met by the beak of ROC 4. ROC 4 clamped his beak down onto Caddy's neck and started pulling the sea serpent out of the water. Caddy reacted with a speed that Bixby and ROC 4 weren't ready for when the monster wrapped his entire body around the giant bird. The sea monster hissed once at the cybernetic bird and then pulled ROC 4 back into the freezing cold water head first. The moment that ROC 4 entered the tank, his beak filled with salt water, choking him. His feathers also filled with water and his steel wings started to pull the monster toward the bottom of the tank. ROC 4 screeched in terror as he was drowning while simultaneously being crushed by Caddy.

Seeing her fiancé in trouble, Munroe had ROC 2 spring into the air. The massive cyborg fluttered over the tank as the thrashing of ROC 4 and Caddy soaked her feathers as well. Munroe had ROC 2 look down to see ROC 4 sinking head first in the tank. She caught a quick glimpse of ROC 4's talon and she urged ROC 2 to grab it. ROC 2's talon shot out and grabbed her mate's talon. Then, in a show of her incredible strength, ROC 2 pulled both the soaked ROC 4 and Caddy out of the tank. ROC 2 flew her mate out from over the tank as Caddy slid away from his body. ROC 2 placed ROC 4 on the ground as Caddy started slithering back toward the bay. ROC 2 made sure that ROC 4 was no longer in distress and then she leapt back into the air. ROC 2 streaked toward the fleeing Caddy, but the monster was able to reach the water before the cybernetic bird could catch him.

Tracy was directing MEG 1 to follow MEG 2 in a tight circle as they swam around the bay. The sharks were circling back toward SeaWorld when a message from Mackenzie flashed in front of her eyes.

ROC 4 is out of commission for the time being. Caddy is headed back to the bay. You guys are up. ROC 2 will provide air support as she can.

Tracy had just finished reading the message when Caddy splashed into the water almost directly on top of MEG 1. Even without Tracy's direction, MEG 1 instinctively snapped her jaws at the sea serpent. Caddy managed to avoid MEG 1's teeth and wrapped himself around the shark's body and tail. Without the use of her tail to propel her through the water, MEG 1 quickly sank to the floor of the bay. With no water moving through her gills, MEG 1 was suffocating. Tracy felt MEG 1 starting to panic. The young doctor had learned from her previous battles rather than letting MEG 1's panic get to her, she directed the shark to unleash a series of electric shocks. MEG 1 compiled and sent thousands of volts of electricity surging into Caddy. The sea serpent writhed in pain for a few seconds before releasing the shark.

Caddy was swimming away from MEG 1 when MEG 2 slammed into the serpentine cryptid jaws first. MEG 2 bit down into Caddy and then he shook his head back and forth. On most opponents, the damage inflicted by a bite from MEG 2 would have killed the creature immediately. Caddy's long body, however, allowed the monster to withstand an extreme amount of punishment.

With his mid-section still in MEG 2's mouth, Caddy swung his head around and bit into MEG 2's back just above his dorsal fin. The two monsters were locked in a stalemate of trying to tear each other in half when Caddy ended the stalemate by slamming his tail into MEG 2's gills. The blow stunned the shark and forced him to release his grip.

Tracy had MEG 1 swimming close to the entangled MEG 2 and Caddy. She had intended to follow Tobias' lead once again and have MEG 1 strike as soon as Caddy was free. When she saw MEG 2 release his bite on Caddy and swim away from the monster, she had MEG 1 charge the sea serpent.

Caddy swung his head around to see MEG 1 coming at him. The cryptid succeeded in moving most of his body out of MEG 1's path, but the shark still managed to sink her teeth into Caddy's tail.

MEG 1 bit down hard on the sea serpent's tail. She then started dragging the cryptid around the bay behind her. The shark gnawed on the monster's tail while simultaneously trying to swing Caddy into a position where she could cut into him with her diamond-coated fins. MEG 1 felt her left pectoral fin slice into Caddy's body when the cryptid suddenly bit down on the base of her tail. The attack surprised both MEG 1 and Tracy, causing the shark to release her grip on Caddy's tail.

The sea monster quickly coiled his body around MEG 1's tail, bringing the shark to bottom of the bay once more. Tracy again responded by having MEG 1 shock the monster until he released his grip on the shark's tail.

Caddy's scales were burned and he was bleeding from several bite wounds. The monster looked to his right to see MEG 2 swimming toward him. Rather than attacking the oncoming shark, Caddy turned and bolted toward the exit of the bay. MEG 2 changed direction to chase after the fleeing creature and MEG 1 quickly joined in the pursuit. Tracy and Tobias were pushing the MEGs as hard as they could, but Caddy was simply faster than the sharks. Tracy gritted her teeth and urged MEG 1 to swim even faster when a message flashed in front of her eyes.

If Caddy makes it back to the open ocean, we are going to lose him! You need to keep him in the bay!

Tracy clenched her fists in anger as she internally thanked Mackenzie for pointing out the obvious. What Tracy didn't realize was the message had been typed not only to her but also to Tobias and Munroe.

ROC 2 was soaring above the bay when Mackenzie's message scrolled across her field of vision. Through ROC 2's eyes, Munroe could see Caddy swimming below the surface of the water. ROC 2 flew past the escaping monster and out over the open ocean. The cybernetic bird then turned around flew toward Caddy. When she was in range of the monster, ROC 2 unleashed a barrage of diamond-coated steel feather at him.

Caddy had nearly reached the open ocean when ROC 2's feathers suddenly rained down on him. The sharp feathers sliced his sides and embedded themselves in his back. The monster hissed in pain. He then slowed down and veered to his right to avoid ROC 2's attack.

When Tobias saw Caddy slowing down and turning, he had MEG 2 change direction to intercept the serpent. Caddy has had just completed veering to his right when MEG 2 clamped his jaws shut around the cryptid's tail. Caddy once more wrapped his body around the shark and constricted it, causing MEG 2 to sink to the bottom of the bay. Tobias could feel MEG 2 starting to panic. The shark was unable to breathe and he needed to escape the monster's grip. Tobias could feel MEG 2 urging him to use the electric shock to force Caddy off him. Despite the shark's anguish, Tobias knew that if he released his grip on Caddy, the game of cat and mouse they were playing in the bay could go on for hours. Tobias did his best to keep the shark calm by reassuring him that MEG 1 and Tracy would figure out what he wanted them to do and put an end to this battle.

When MEG 1 reached the entangled Caddy and MEG 2, Tracy had her shark swim a holding pattern around the two monsters. Her plan was to wait for MEG 1 to shock Caddy off himself and then to try and attack the elusive monster once again. After swimming two circles around the struggling monsters, Tracy wondered why Tobias had not yet forced Caddy to release MEG 2 as the shark was clearly in distress.

Tracy quickly saw that Tobias was holding Caddy in place because he wanted MEG 1 to do something. Tracy took a deep breath and tried to see the situation through Tobias' eyes. She had MEG 1 focus her sight on Caddy and MEG 2 and an idea formed in her head. She thought to herself. *He wants MEG 1 to execute a surgical attack. To take out Caddy without hurting MEG 2.* Tracy knew that such an attack would require speed and precision. She could also see that MEG 2's struggles were weakening from his inability to breathe.

Tracy had MEG 1 swim away from the two monsters. She then directed the shark to turn around and swim toward Caddy and MEG 2 at top speed. MEG 1 was a massive creature who primarily used her size and bulk to defeat her opponents. She was designed to slam her bulk into her prey in order to stun it. Tracy was now trying to take that same size and bulk to use her right pectoral fin to slice into Caddy without injuring the shark he was wrapped around.

As MEG 1 was swimming toward Caddy and MEG 2, she urged the shark to make subtle shifts in her approach. Tracy was sweating as she knew that if she were off in her approach by only a few feet that she could inadvertently kill not only MEG 2 but Tobias as well. Just prior to making contact with Caddy and MEG 2, Tracy had MEG 1 shift her weight to the left. The slight movement worked as Tracy felt MEG 1's pectoral fin slice through Caddy's spine.

Tracy had MEG 1 turn around to see the two halves of Caddy's body floating in a cloud of blood. She also saw MEG 2 swim out of the crimson mist with a slight cut on his side. From what Tracy could tell, the wound was superficial as MEG 2 seemed to be swimming without issue.

The blood in the water sent MEG 1 into a feeding a frenzy. The shark shifted her body in the direction of the upper half of Caddy's body. Tracy pulled the neurolink off her head so she would not share MEG 1's experience of devouring the dead cryptid.

As Tracy sat up in her recliner, she could still feel the primal urges that accompanied being linked to a giant monster in battle welling up inside of her. This time, she was prepared for the urges and she was able to conduct herself with a greater degree of control than she had upon exiting previous battles. Her urges were also tempered by her concern over Tobias nearly being strangled to death when he was synced with MEG 2.

Tracy ran over to Tobias as he was pulling off his neurolink helmet. She quickly ran over and kissed him. She pulled her lips away from Tobias and looked down at him with concern. "Are you okay? MEG 2 nearly suffocated. Then I cut into his side when attacking Caddy." Tracy's eyes suddenly went wide. "That was what you wanted me to do, wasn't it?"

Tobias smiled. "I'm fine, and so is MEG 2. That cut looks painful, but it's really not that bad, and yes, that's exactly what I wanted you to do." He climbed out of his recliner and hugged Tracy. "When I had MEG 2 hold Caddy in place, I had total faith in you to figure out how to end the fight."

Tracy smiled. "I guess we really are getting to know each other better." She kissed Tobias again and then looked over at Mackenzie. "How are ROC 2 and ROC 4?"

Mackenzie looked up from his computer screen. "Both ROCs are fine, as are Munroe and Bixby. ROC 4 will need to dry out for a few hours before he is able to fly, so he and ROC 2 are going to stay in SeaWorld for a while. After the MEGs finish eating, you two will briefly need to sync up with them and send them across the Pacific. Your next objective is to engage Otaka off the coast of Japan."

Jillian yelled from behind her computer screen, "Mackenzie, we have a problem." Mackenzie, Tracy, and Tobias all walked over to Jillian's computer screen to see a dot moving across it. She pointed to the dot. "The Shojo is heading directly for Toamasina, Madagascar."

CHAPTER 14
TOAMASINA, MADAGASCAR

General Tochi Ibaka was sitting in his office when he received the call from the president that the U.S. had informed him the Shojo was headed to Toamasina, the chief port city of the island nation. Tochi's first question was if the ROCs would be able to help in the defense of the city. When the president responded that the ROCs would be unable to assist in the battle against the Shojo, Tochi immediately suggested the president's best course of action was to order a mass evacuation of Toamasina.

Given the scope of such an evacuation and the short amount of time they had until the Shojo made landfall, the president was initially resistant to the idea. Tochi then quickly reviewed how the Shojo had decimated the U.S. naval base at Diego Garcia and how the monster withstood attacks from warships at point-blank range. After considering these facts, the president reconsidered his position.

Tochi was now sitting inside the mobile headquarters on the docks of the city. The command center had the shape of a massive RV but inside, it was fully equipped to run a tactical operation. The command center was heavily armored. It was capable of withstanding cannon fire while still retaining operational capability. In addition to three hundred and sixty degrees worth of cameras, the mobile command center also had a small platform that ran all around it to allow officers to view a battle firsthand.

It had been three hours since the president had ordered Toamasina evacuated. All roads and rail lines into and out of the city were opened for evacuees. The entire bus and train fleet of the public transportation system was put into full effect. Tochi was reviewing the progress of the evacuation. He was pleased that overall the city evacuation was going as well as could be hoped for. Conversely, he was also concerned that only twenty percent of the city had been evacuated with the Shojo due to reach the city within a few minutes.

Tochi walked out of the mobile command center to see an array of PT-76 light tanks and armored cars pulled up to the harbor and waiting for the monster to make his appearance. Tochi had no delusions about how the upcoming encounter was going to play out. His forces didn't stand a chance against the monster that was heading toward them. If warships were unable to injure the Shojo then tanks and armored vehicles would be woefully inadequate to make a stand against him. All that Tochi could do was to try and provide the people of Toamasina a few more minutes to evacuate the city.

A screeching sound echoed through the sky above Tochi's head and he looked up to see five MIG-17s flying overhead. The fighters were circling the city and waiting for Tochi's command to attack. Tochi walked back into the mobile command station and approached the radar display. He tapped the soldier who was watching the radar on the shoulder. "How much longer until the Shojo is visible from the shoreline?"

The soldier kept his eyes focused on the radar. "The monster should be breaching the water in less than one minute, sir."

Tochi took a deep breath and grabbed his radio. "This is General Ibaka. All fighters, move into position to make your bombing run."

A solemn voice replied, "Copy that, sir."

Tochi walked outside to see the fighters circle over the city and then fly out toward the bay. Tochi brought his binoculars to his eyes and he looked out over the bay at a massive swell of water that was entering the harbor. The general quickly set the timer on his watch, and then looked back through his binoculars to see a hairy face breaking through the top of the swell. Tochi was a lifelong military man. He had seen many horrible things over the course of his career, but nothing compared to the horrific sight of the Shojo's face. Tochi saw a head that had a similar shape to an orangutan's skull. Despite the creature's wide skull, its face possessed a disturbing human-like quality. The Shojo's face was covered in fur and long fangs protruded out from its jaws, and yet the creature's face still reminded the general of a human being. The Shojo's face reminded Tochi of the way Lon Chaney's face looked like after he had transformed into the Wolfman.

The Shojo's shoulder rose out of the water as the MIGs approached the monster. Tochi watched as the MIGs dropped a torrent of bombs onto the man-beast. The water around the Shojo and the monster himself were engulfed in flames as shockwaves from the explosions shook the harbor. The general heard a collective cheer from the ground forces waiting at the water's edge. They had thought the initial bombing run had destroyed the creature, but Tochi knew better. His fears were confirmed when a loud roar came from within the smoke-blanketed bay.

The Shojo walked out through the cloud of smoke and continued his march toward Toamasina. Rol-Hama's command to destroy was still running through the Shojo's mind. The command was a like a primal urge that was only quenched when the cryptid was tearing something apart. At first, this new desire was easily quenched by attacking the countless ships that sailed across the ocean. When the ships stopped appearing on the water, the Shojo felt compelled to find other targets on which to unleash his anger. He had first attacked the naval base and that briefly satisfied the urge deep within him, but the urge quickly returned. Typically, the Shojo despised leaving the water, but Rol-Hama's command to destroy was unrelenting. The Shojo saw the brightly lit city ahead of him as a target he could vent his frustrations on and soothe the urge within him.

Tochi watched the MIGs circling back toward the Shojo as the monster continued his march toward the city. This time, the jets attacked the monster from behind. The MIGs fired on the Shojo with missiles and high-caliber bullets, all of which had no effect on the approaching horror. The jets flew past the Shojo and back out over the city. They were circling back around to attack again when Tochi noticed how close the Shojo was to shore. He feared that if the jets attacked again, they might inadvertently hit the ground forces with friendly fire. He quickly grabbed his radio. "This is General Ibaka. All MIGs are to return to base. Ground forces, prepare to open fire on my mark!"

Tochi quickly glanced down at his watch to see that only ninety-six seconds had passed since the Shojo first broke the surface of the water. He cursed at the thought that his first wave of defense had already been spent and he had only managed to give the people evacuating the city an extra minute and a half.

Tochi dropped his binoculars to the ground as the Shojo was close enough to shore that even his nearsighted eyes could clearly see the colossus. The Shojo had made his way to hip-deep water and he was still progressing toward the city. The monster took several more steps forward and when he was within range of the armored vehicles on shore, Tochi yelled into his radio. "Ground forces, open fire!" The mobile command center shook as tanks and armored vehicles opened fire on the approaching Gargantua. Tochi looked on as missiles, shells, tracer rounds, and rockets all exploded against the Shojo. For a brief moment, the barrage caused the monster to halt his forward progress and place his arm in front of his face.

When Tochi saw the monster stop moving forward, he committed the mistake of allowing hope to creep into his mind. That hope was quickly dashed to pieces as the Shojo roared and then continued moving forward. Tochi knew what was going to happen next. The Shojo was going to tear through the ground forces as if they were insects trying to impede a charging elephant. When the Shojo stepped out of the water, the impact of his massive foot slamming into the ground knocked several of the armored vehicles on their sides.

Tochi then watched in horror as the Shojo crouched down and began smashing the soldiers who were opposing him to a pulp. Despite the horror he was witnessing, Tochi felt pride in the fact that not one of his soldiers turned and ran. Each one of them knew he was facing certain death and yet every man continued to fire at the monster until he was crushed to death by the Shojo's fury. Tochi watched helplessly as the aquatic ape lifted his hands into the air and repeatedly brought them crashing down into his forces. With each blow, the monster crushed multiple vehicles and killed dozens of men. When the monster had finally killed the last of his soldiers, Tochi looked back down at the timer he started at the onset of the battle. Tochi shook his head when he saw that the timer was only at three minutes and forty-five seconds.

Tochi watched as the Shojo stood up and lifted his blood-soaked hand into the air. The Shojo roared and then he started moving toward the buildings directly in front of him. Tochi once more lifted his radio to his mouth. "Wave three, move into position!"

Tochi looked down the main street leading to the harbor to see not tanks and armored trucks moving toward the Shojo but police vehicles. He then shifted his eyes up to see the tops of the buildings that lined the waterfront. Tochi nodded his head in approval as dozens of police officers suddenly appeared on rooftops. Once he saw that everyone was in position, Tochi yelled into his radio. "Wave three, attack!"

Tochi watched as the massed police officers lifted large guns into the air. Loud popping sounds came from the streets and rooftops as the officers fired every canister of tear gas within the city limits at the Shojo. The officers on the street fired at the monster's legs while those on the rooftops fired at the cryptid's face. Tochi heard the Shojo shriek in pain as the burning white gas worked its way into the monster's eyes, nose, ears, and mouth. The cloud of tear gas started to shift away from the Shojo and toward the harbor. Tochi saw the gas coming toward him so he ran back into the mobile command center and closed its door. He then ran over to the nearest external visual feed to see the effect his last line of defense had on the Shojo.

Currently, the visual feed was only showing the cloud of tear gas that was clinging to the Shojo. While Tochi couldn't see the monster, he could still hear the Shojo's screams. Tochi smiled and pumped his fists at the realization that he finally hurt the beast.

With the cloud of tear gas slowly clearing, Tochi could see the Shojo clawing at his face in an attempt to remove the painful gas that was seeping into his orifices. Tochi's eyes lit up when he saw the Shojo turn and run. The general felt the ground beneath the mobile command center bouncing up and down. The feed on the display screen switched to another view when the Shojo ran past the mobile command center and leapt back into the bay.

The men in the mobile center cheered as the Shojo disappeared in the estuary. They turned to each other and started exchanging handshakes and hugs. Tochi was the only person who maintained his composure. He called out to those around him, "Stay focused! We don't know if this battle is over yet!"

At the command of their general, the soldiers immediately calmed down and returned to their stations. Tochi watched the video feed of the bay and of the cloud of tear gas that covered the harbor. The wind from the harbor was quickly dispersing the cloud and that worried the hardened general. The cloud of tear gas had nearly completely dissipated when an enraged Shojo shot up out of the water. The monster shrieked and then started making his way back to shore and directly for the mobile command center.

Tochi continued to watch the video feed as the Shojo's huge hairy hand reached for the command center. Tochi caught a brief glimpse of the monster's hand filling up the display screen before the entire command center was lifted into the air. When the command center finally stopped moving higher, Tochi quickly looked at his timer to see that it read seven minutes and twenty-four seconds. He guessed that in that timeframe, at least three more trains full of people were able to make it out of the city. Tochi closed his eyes and told himself that he did all he could. The thought had barely managed to cross his mind when the Shojo hurled the command center into the heart of the city. As he was in free fall, Tochi managed to say a brief prayer for the safety of his family before the mobile command center crashed into a building, killing him and everyone else inside.

After tossing the mobile center into the heart of the city, the Shojo climbed back on shore. The police officers who were still gathered in the streets and on top of buildings fired on the beast with shotguns and handguns. The Shojo walked through the small arms attack without even noticing it. The cryptid walked up to the building directly in front of him and drove his fist through it, causing its top half to crumble to the streets below. The simian horror kicked the lower half of the building several times, reducing it to dust. The Shojo roared again and then attacked the building next to him.

Two hours later, fifteen blocks were reduced to rubble and the urge to destroy implanted in the Shojo by the maniacal Rol-Hama had finally been quenched. The Shojo turned and looked upon the devastation he had wrought. The monster roared once again and then he headed back to the ocean where he would rest until the need to destroy overwhelmed him   again.

CHAPTER 15
BALTIMORE

Tracy and Tobias had enjoyed a twenty-four-hour respite after their battle with Caddy. After working off some of the emotions they had carried over from syncing with the MEGs during a battle, they slept the rest of the night. The next morning, they did what all couples need to do every so often and spent some time apart. They knew that if they were to grow as a couple that maintaining a sense of individual identity outside of the relationship was also important. Tracy enjoyed her time by reviewing some of the latest journal articles in neuroscience and then by going off base and hitting the karaoke bar she mentioned to Tobias for a few hours. Tobias filled his time by putting in a request for a jet plane and taking it for a long flight. For the pilot who had spent so much time connected to a monster that lived underwater, getting back into the sky was a relaxing and rejuvenating experience.

When the two of them met outside of the briefing room for a meeting with Mackenzie, they smiled and hugged each other. They then walked into the briefing room to find not only George Mackenzie and Jillian Crean waiting for them, but also the President of United States on the large display screen.

Tobias quickly saluted the president and Tracy did the same. She wasn't sure if she had to salute the president, but she felt it was a case of better safe than sorry. The president smiled at the MEG pilots. "Dr. Curry, Captain Crow, you two are doing some fine work out there. Mr. Mackenzie has told me that you two have already eliminated three of the five monsters who have been plaguing our oceans?"

Tobias nodded. "Yes, sir. That is correct."

The president nodded. "That's excellent. Keep up the good work." He then turned to look at Mackenzie. "Now, what in the hell happened in Madagascar? I've got their president calling me and saying that one of his major cities was decimated and thousands of people were killed because the ROCs were not there to fight off the Shojo?"

Mackenzie shrugged. "It was my call, sir. We had Caddy in SeaWorld and I felt we needed to address a known threat on U.S. soil as quickly and as effectively as possible. As such, I directed the ROCs to California to deal with Caddy rather than to wait for a potential attack somewhere in the Indian Ocean." He looked into the president's eyes. "It was a gamble that cost the people of Madagascar dearly, but given the same situation again, I would have made the same call. I will accept whatever consequences you see fit for my decision."

The president shook his head. "Hell, George, that was a tough call either way. We can evaluate your command decisions when this whole thing is over. I also understand that the giant octopus has attacked a bridge in Japan. How long is it until the ROCs are combat ready and the MEGs engage the next target? Also, can we expect to see more attacks on land from these monsters in the meantime?"

Mackenzie brought a world map onto the screen showing two red dots moving together across the Pacific Ocean toward Japan, one green dot moving into the Pacific from the coast of Japan, two blue dots over the Atlantic Ocean, and one green dot in the middle of the Indian Ocean. Mackenzie highlighted the green dots first. "The green dots represent the Shojo and Otaka. The blue dots represent the ROCs and the red dots represent the MEGs. The good news is that both ROCs are fully functional and should reach Tanzania in two hours. That will put them back on the outskirts of the Shojo's territory. The issue we are running into now is that without any ships on the ocean the monsters seem to be looking for other targets to attack. This drive is leading them to attack sites on or near the shore or to attack other large creatures in their territory. That would explain why the Shojo, Otaka, and Caddy attacked the sites they did and why the Mermaid and Trunko attacked the MEGs when the sharks entered their territory. In some cases where the monster attacks the MEGs, it's to our benefit. This way, the MEGs targets are focused on the sharks and not on land targets. It also reduces time between targets when the monster swims out to meet the MEGs as opposed to having to hunt them down." Mackenzie highlighted the green dot in the Pacific. "As you can see, Otaka is currently swimming out to meet the MEGs. We project the MEGs will engage Otaka in the middle of the Pacific Ocean in less than eight hours."

The president nodded. "That's good, but what about the Shojo? He represents a much more dangerous threat to land-based cities than the octopus does. Can the ROCs engage him if need be?"

Mackenzie nodded. "We can track the Shojo's movements and have the ROCs shadow him if he tries to make landfall again. This monster seems to be pretty smart though. The last time he encountered the ROCs, he swam to the middle of the ocean and waited for the ROCs to tire and fly back to land before moving again. It's entirely possible for the ROCs to dissuade any land attacks from the Shojo, but the MEGs will have to be the ones to take him out for good."

Mackenzie brought an image of a large boat onto the screen. "We do, however, have a plan to distract the Shojo and start leading him toward the MEGs, assuming of course the MEGs are successful in killing Otaka. This is one of two Sea Hunter drone ships we currently have docked off the coast of South Africa. The Sea Hunters are fully armed naval drones capable of reaching the speed of our top destroyers. The drones can be piloted remotely and are light enough that one of ROCs can carry them in the air. Currently, the Shojo is resting off the coast of Madagascar. I propose we have the ROCs pick up these drones and drop them in areas where they will gain the attention of the Shojo. The drones will then lead him into an encounter with the MEGs, thereby reducing the chance of any more land attacks."

Mackenzie stopped for a moment and took a drink of water, partially because he was thirsty and also to let the president process what he had said. Mackenzie put his water down and continued. "We know the Shojo's top speed in the water is more the double the top speed of the drones. In order for this plan to work, will need ROC 2 to fly the first drone to an area on the Indian Ocean within fifty miles of the Shojo. Once the Shojo starts giving chase, we will have the drone move at top speed toward Australia. We calculate the Shojo will catch the first drone and destroy it somewhere in the middle of the Indian Ocean. When that happens, ROC 4 will fly the second drone fifty miles away from the Shojo and toward Australia and then the second leg of our chase begins. We calculate this chase will end off the northern coast of Australia. Once the Shojo reaches that point, we hope the MEGs will have defeated Otaka and the Shojo will sense their presence. If he continues to act in the manner he has thus far, we hope to have the MEGs engaged with him in the Timor Sea within twenty-two hours."

Mackenzie looked at the president. "Sir, with your approval of this plan, we hope to have this entire crisis ended within twenty-four hours."

The president nodded. "That's a hell of an ambitious plan, Director." The president then looked over at Tracy and Tobias. "Captain Crow, Dr. Curry, are the two of you and the MEGs ready to fight two monsters in one day?"

Tracy and Tobias responded with a simultaneous. "Yes, sir."

The president smiled. "All right then. Director Mackenzie, you have my approval to move ahead with this plan. Go kick some sea monster ass."

The president cut off the feed from his end. Mackenzie grabbed his phone and started making calls to get the ROCs and drones into place.

Jillian Crean who had sat silently throughout the meeting stood and walked over to Tracy and Tobias. When she reached them, she grabbed each of them by the hand. "Listen, you know those calculations could change or the MEGs may need you after the battle with Otaka." She squeezed their hands. "There is very good chance that you two won't be able to unsync with the MEGs until this mission is over. Is that something you are ready for?"

Tracy looked over at Tobias. She could see a hard stoic look on his face and she knew what was bothering him. She squeezed his hand and then looked back at Jillian. "We can do this, Jillian."

Jillian nodded. "Okay, I'd say you two have roughly five hours until we need you to sync with MEGs. Go and enjoy some time to yourselves for a while then meet us in the neurolink room to put an end to this nightmare."

Tracy nodded and then turned and pulled Tobias out of the room. She continued to hold his hand as they walked back to their quarters. When they entered their quarters, Tracy sat Tobias down on the couch and placed her head on his shoulder. She spoke softly and calmly. "It's okay if you are still concerned about facing the Shojo. You won't be alone this time. We will be facing him together as a team."

Tobias leaned his head into her. "I know you'll be there. It's just I can't shake that feeling of ROC 1 dying as we fought the Sasquatch. I can't explain to you what it's like to be connected with another living being as they are dying and knowing how I let him down. It was horrible enough to feel ROC 1 dying, but what made it worse was the feeling he knew that I never let him in. Every time I synced with ROC 1, he wanted to be a part of me and I wouldn't let him. He died knowing the one being on the planet that he wanted to be connected was never going to let him in." He shook his head. "I've heard people talk about Post-Traumatic Stress Disorder. I think I might have it. When I see the Shojo, in my head he changes into the Sasquatch and all those feelings of death, loss, and disappointment ROC 1 had as he died come rushing back into my mind."

Tracy lifted her head up and she looked into Tobias' eyes. "I don't know if this sounds heartless or not, but it's the only way I can think to say it." She swallowed hard. "Maybe your experience with ROC 1's death will turn out to be a positive thing, not just for you, but for the world. If you hadn't felt what ROC 1 felt as he died, would you be as open about your feelings as you are now? You have said you are syncing with MEG 2 at a far deeper level than you did with ROC 1. Would you be able to let yourself sync so well with another monster if it wasn't for

ROC 1's death? If you weren't able to sync so deeply with MEG 2, would our mission already have failed and have left the human race facing its most difficult time since the last Ice Age?"

She leaned in a little closer to Tobias. "If you hadn't have felt the disappointment and loneliness that ROC 1 felt, would have been open to taking a chance with me? Would you have let me into your life to see who you are? Who you really are?" She shrugged. "ROC 1's death may have saved me as well. Without you, I don't know that I ever would have fallen in love. I may have gone through my entire life with no one to hold onto to. No one to share my fears and joys with like I have with you over the past few months?" Tracy started to tear up. "Is it possible to look at ROC 1's death not as that of a creature who died in despair but rather as a noble being whose sacrifice brought us together? Whose death gave us the strength to finish the war that you and he entered into over a year ago?" She shook her head. "I don't want to diminish the tragedy of ROC 1's death, I just want to emphasize how it's possible to draw some positives from it."

Tobias kissed her and then he held her head in his hands as he talked to her. "You're right. I may have failed ROC 1 by not letting him in when he died, but I learned from his death and became a better person going forward. Maybe I need to stop beating myself up over failing him and start focusing how I can make sure I don't fail the people I have let into my life." He kissed Tracy again. "I just hope that I can keep it together when we face the Shojo."

Tracy smiled. "You will. I know you will. I know you will because you are Tobias Crow and because you are the man I love." Tracy wiped a tear from her eye. "Right now, we have to rest though. Before we even worry about the Shojo, we have a giant octopus to fight. If we don't focus on him first, he could very well kill the MEGs and end our mission."

Tobias nodded. "You're right. Let's get some sleep." He looked around the room. "I am warning you now though. Hopefully, the next chance we will have to be in this room will be when this war is over, and if it is, we won't be sleeping."

CHAPTER 16
INDIAN OCEAN OFF THE COAST OF MADAGASCAR

The Shojo sat on the bottom of the ocean floor, chewing on the remains of a sperm whale he had captured. The monster rolled over as he felt the anger and aggression beginning to build within him once more. It had been over a day and a half since he had gone ashore and destroyed Toamasina. After laying waste to the city and returning to the ocean, the aquatic ape felt a sense of calm for several hours. That serene feeling was slowly being eroded away by the implants Rol-Hama had placed in his body. The Shojo was starting to consider going ashore to attack another city when his seemingly supernatural senses detected something on the ocean.

The beast closed his eyes and focused on the miniscule vibrations he was feeling through the water. The Shojo sifted through the vibrations being given off by sea life and volcanic activity and focused on the one vibration that was different from the rest. The Shojo roared at the thought of another ship sailing across his waters. The ship was far off, but the monster was confident that he could catch it. The monster was suddenly filled with the desire to destroy the man made vehicle. He roared once more as he leapt off the ocean floor and began pursuing the newest target of his manufactured rage.

****

ROC 2 had just deposited the Sea Hunter in the ocean when a message flashed across Munroe's field of vision.

The Shojo is pursuing target. Return to base immediately. We don't want ROC 2's presence to scare him off.

The message then disappeared and Munroe directed ROC 2 to return to her temporary base in Africa.

****

Tracy and Tobias didn't wait for an alarm to wake them and send them sprinting down to the neurolink room. They arrived an hour earlier than their scheduled time in order to sync with the cybernetic sharks prior to engaging Otaka in battle. As usual, Mackenzie and Jillian were already at their computers, preparing the neurolink for the upcoming mission.

Tobias walked Tracy over to her neurolink recliner. Before she sat down in it, she whispered into his ear. "For once, I get to tell you that we can do this." Tobias smiled and kissed her. She then sat down in her recliner and watched Tobias walk over to his neurolink connection. She watched him put his helmet on and then she placed her own helmet over her head.

Tracy saw the now familiar flash of light and then she found herself looking at the endless ocean. Tracy was so well connected to MEG 1 at this point that she could sense the shark's awareness of her. She could sense that MEG 1 was happy to be reconnected with her. Tracy felt the same way and made sure that MEG 1 understood her feelings as well. As the extended final mission loomed ahead of her, Tracy considered all that her time with MEG 1 had let her experience. She reflected on the fact that she had been able to explore the ocean in a way no other human being had ever done before her. She was able to swim through the deepest depths of the world's oceans and not only see the wonders it held, but smell them, taste them, and feel them with an extra sense that no other human would ever experience.

Tracy focused on MEG 1's mind and thought, *No matter the outcome of our upcoming battles, I want you to know how grateful I am to you for allowing me to understand the ocean in the same way you do. Thank you, my friend. Whatever happens when this is all over, you will always be a part of me.* Tracy smiled as she felt a similar sentiment filter through MEG 1's mind in relation to her.

Tracy and MEG 1 swam for another half an hour before the super shark's electroreception senses picked up a colossal creature moving toward her. Tracy saw MEG 2 swim up beside her and she knew that he sensed the presence as well.

MEG 1's electroreception sense was indicating that whatever was heading toward the sharks was massive. Tracy was trying to remember the initial details from the briefing on all of the monsters when text started to appear across her field of vision.

Otaka is an over five hundred foot wide octopus when his tentacles are fully extended. In addition to his strength and bulk, each of his tentacles is covered with hundreds of suckers. Each of the suckers hold hooks the size of a cruise ship anchor. They are powerful enough to penetrate the MEGs' hides. Try to avoid them if you can by attacking his head from above.

Tracy briefly wondered how she was supposed to have MEG 1 avoid tentacles longer than a football field while also attacking the monster. A huge black shadow suddenly appeared in water in front of MEG 1. The shadow slowly morphed into the form of an octopus as it swam toward the sharks. Tracy's body shook when Otaka threw his tentacles out in front of himself and started undulating them back and forth. When she saw the giant cephalopod arm's fully extended, Tracy was in awe of how large the monster actually was. Ever since she had first synced with MEG 1, Tracy felt as if she was connected to the largest and most powerful creature in the ocean. As she stared at Otaka, she realized that her claim to being the biggest monster on the planet had been demonstrably falsified.

Tracy could feel MEG 1 reacting to her apprehension and she did her best to exude confidence and reassure the shark that they could defeat this creature. Both Tracy and MEG 1's confidence was reassured when MEG 2 swam past them to engage the cryptid. Tracy knew that MEG 2's attack was a ploy. She had MEG 1 swim up a little to attack Otaka from above while MEG 2 distracted him with a head-on charge.

MEG 2 had almost reached Otaka when the cephalopod's tentacles shot out and swatted the shark aside as if he were a minnow. MEG 1 shifted her eyes for a moment to see MEG 2 tumbling through the water. Tracy then had MEG 1 look back toward Otaka to see a wall of tentacles reaching out for her.

MEG 1 was suddenly caught in a constricting grip that was far stronger than either Trunko's trunk or Caddy's body. The pain MEG 1 was feeling from being crushed was nothing compared to the pain of her scales being ripped to shreds by the hooks hidden within Otaka's suckers.

The pain MEG 1 was experiencing was so intense that it caused Tracy to scream. Jillian ran over to her friend as Tracy continued to scream and her body convulsed. Jillian looked down at Tracy's face to see tears streaming down her cheeks. She was about to pull the neurolink helmet off Tracy's head when Mackenzie yelled, "No! Leave it on her! MEG 1 is going to need her input if she is going to survive this fight!" Jillian glared at Mackenzie and then she slowly backed away from her friend.

Tobias saw a cloud of blood forming around MEG 1 and he urged MEG 2 to attack Otaka again. MEG 2 swam at Otaka with his mouth open. When he reached the huge octopus, the shark clamped his jaws shut around the base of one of the tentacles that was wrapped around his mate. MEG 2 was tearing into the appendage when several other tentacles ensnared him as well. The tentacles immediately tightened and a second later, MEG 2 was in the same agony as MEG 1 from the tearing action of Otaka's hooks.

MEG 1 shook her body back and forth as she tried to break free of Otaka's grip. The shark was in such excruciating pain that she was inhibiting Tracy's ability to think and focus on how to escape the death grip. Tracy was still screaming in pain when through MEG 1, she felt an electric shock. The slight shock was enough to break MEG 1's mind from solely focusing on the pain and allow Tracy to think about what was going on. Tracy felt another shock and she realized that it was coming from MEG 2 as Tobias continued to use the shark's electric charge to break free of Otaka's grip. Tracy gritted her teeth and focused on having MEG 1 engage her own electric charge.

The combined voltage coming off the two MEGs was too much for Otaka. The octopus released his grip and tried to swim away from the sharks. As Otaka pulled his hooks out of the MEGs, each hook tore a huge chunk of scales away with it. MEG 1 shifted her eyes toward MEG 2. Tracy gasped when she saw huge bleeding wounds all over the shark's body. From the wall of blood that was clouding her field of vision, Tracy knew that MEG 1 was covered in similar wounds.

Otaka was still moving away from the cybernetic sharks when MEG 2 shot forward and bit down on one of his tentacles. MEG 2 tore into the tentacle with the ferocity of a rabid pit bull. Within seconds of biting into the tentacle, MEG 2 tore the appendage off the octopus. The monstrous shark swallowed one bite of the appendage and then continued to press his attack.

Tracy saw two more tentacles moving toward MEG 1 from above. The young doctor directed MEG 1 to dive and thrust her dorsal fin upward. The diamond-coated steel fin sliced through two of the tentacles, severing them off. In a reflexive motion, Otaka's five remaining tentacles reached out and grabbed the two MEGs. Once more, the sharks and the pilots were subjected to the horrible pain of Otaka's hooks tearing into their skin. Both Tracy and Tobias had the MEGs activate their electric shocks the moment that Otaka wrapped his tentacles around them. The shocks caused the monster to pull his tentacles off the sharks, once again tearing huge pieces of flesh from the MEGs. Tracy could sense that MEG 1 was being severely injured by the suckers, but she urged the shark to fight through the pain and continue her attack. Tracy's body shook once more as she felt a long strip of scales peeled off MEG 1's back.

Tracy saw Otaka backing away and she urged MEG 1 to move forward and attack. She knew the sooner this battle ended, the more likely it was that MEG 1 would survive it. MEG 1 swam forward and leaned her left pectoral fin into one of Otaka's tentacles, slicing it in half. She then closed her jaws on another tentacle and bit it off. MEG 2 also pushed forward, slicing off one of Otaka's tentacles with his dorsal fin and biting off another.

The mortally wounded octopus wrapped his last remaining tentacle around MEG 1, once more using his hooks to slice into the cyborg's scales. Tracy had MEG 1 engage her electric shock again as MEG 2 slammed into Otaka's head teeth first. Otaka released his grip on MEG 1 and she closed her jaws on the tentacle and tore it off. MEG 1's eyes rolled over to see MEG 2 wounded badly but still tearing into Otaka's head. MEG 1 swam through a cloud of her own blood and joined MEG 2 in tearing what was left of Otaka to pieces.

The sharks were devouring the remains of Otaka when Tracy saw text scroll across her field of vision.

Disengage from the neurolink now!

Tracy pulled her helmet off her head. As usual, she was happy that she didn't have to stay connected to the shark while she fed and she was also happy to no longer feel the pain MEG 1 was enduring from the wounds Otaka had inflicted.

Tracy looked over at Tobias and from the way he was moving, she could tell that he felt a lot of pain from MEG 2's wounds as well. Tracy was starting to climb out of her recliner when she heard Mackenzie screaming, "I told you two to attack the octopus from above! What the hell part of that didn't you understand?"

Tracy jumped out of her recliner and screamed at Mackenzie, "There was no way that plan was going work! There was no way of getting around those tentacles! The only way to kill that octopus was to go through them!" She was going to scream at Mackenzie more when Tobias grabbed her hand.

Tobias looked past Mackenzie and at Jillian Crean. "How badly injured are they?"

Jillian shook her head. "Both MEGs have lost nearly fifty percent of their outer scales. Even with their advanced healing abilities, the damage is too great. They are losing blood faster than their bodies can heal their wounds." Jillian walked over and put her hands on Tracy's and Tobias' shoulders. "Their healing abilities will buy them some time, but at best, both MEGs will die within twelve hours."

CHAPTER 17
INDIAN OCEAN

The Shojo could see the ship moving on the surface of the water above him. The strange beast moved through the ocean at a speed that belied his morphology and size. The Shojo's horrific face surfaced behind the Sea Hunter. The aquatic ape roared at the drone that had dared to invade his territory and then he closed in on it. The sailors who were piloting the Sea Hunter saw the approaching monster on their rearview cameras and they armed the drone accordingly.

The Shojo had nearly reached the Sea Hunter when the drone fired twin torpedoes at it. The torpedoes skimmed across the surface of the water and then exploded in the Shojo's face. The monster shrieked in pain as the flash from the explosion burned his mouth and teeth. The Shojo shook his head to clear his vision and then he started swimming toward the drone again. The Sea Hunter fired another round of torpedoes at the Shojo, but the monster swatted them aside, causing them to detonate several hundred feet to his left. With a few more quick strokes, the rage-filled Shojo caught the fleeing Sea Hunter. The kaiju closed his claws around the Sea Hunter and crushed the high-tech drone. The beast roared in victory and then he slipped back beneath the waves.

Fifty miles northeast of the Shojo's position, ROC 4 was circling over the ocean with the second Sea Hunter in his claws. Bixby was piloting the cybernetic bird when he saw a message flash before his eyes.

Sea Hunter 1 has been destroyed. Drop Sea Hunter 2 in target area and return to base.

Bixby had ROC 4 carry out Mackenzie's orders. When the second Sea Hunter was placed on the ocean, it began heading toward Australia at top speed. Fifty miles away, the Shojo sensed the boat's movement. The anger and urge to destroy placed in the beast by Rol-Hama started to build once more. The monster roared and then he began swimming toward his new target.

BALTIMORE

Upon hearing the news of the MEGs impending death, the two pilots reacted in vastly different manners. Tobias simply sat down on a nearby chair and placed his hands over his face. Rife with thoughts about the death of ROC 1, the hardened Air Force pilot did his best to keep himself from breaking down into tears.

Tracy Curry stood silently staring at Mackenzie and Jillian Crean. Her body began to shake and her eyes filled up with tears. Her lower lip began to tremble, and then finally she started to scream, "She can't be dying! There's gotta be something we can do!" She looked over at Jillian. "Don't just stand there looking at me! Find a bay or something that we can direct the MEGs to. We've already saved the damn world twice! One of the other countries in the world has to be able to help us!" She turned and ran over to the computer that Jillian was using to track the MEGs. She quickly scanned the screen to see where the MEGs were in relation to the closest possible help. Tracy pointed at the screen. "Tokyo Bay! We are less than twenty miles from Tokyo Bay! Japan has some of the best marine biologists in the world and their robotics program is second to none! There has to be people there who can save the MEGs!" Tracy ran over and grabbed her lover's hand. "Come on, Tobias!" We can make it to Tokyo Bay!" She looked over at Mackenzie. "Call in some of those favors the world owes you. Get a team of people into the bay who can help heal the MEGs!"

Tracy pulled on Tobias' arm, but he didn't move. She glared down at him. "Tobias, come on! The sooner we can get the MEGs to Tokyo Bay, the better the chances are of saving them!" Tears ran down Tracy's face as she looked at Tobias.

Tobias wiped his eyes clean as he looked into the face of the woman he loved. "Tracy, I could sense it from MEG 2 when I was still connected to him. He's hurt too bad. Even if he was close to Baltimore, I don't think there's anything that we could do to save him." He stood up and looked into Tracy's eyes. "Be honest with yourself, did you get the same feeling from MEG 1?"

Tracy stared at Tobias and shook her head. There was another moment of eerie silence before Tracy started screaming again, "NO! I can't accept that! We've been through too much together! A few weeks ago, I could barely swim through the water without nearly having her kill herself! Now I feel her desires and pains as if they were my own! I can't lose her now! I can't!" She quieted down, placed her head on Tobias' shoulder, and wept.

Mackenzie walked over to them and placed his hand on Tracy's shoulder. "Tracy, it's always difficult when you lose a member of your unit. When you fight alongside someone, they become like members of your family. Closer than your family even. Tobias will tell you though, when you are soldier, the mission always comes first. Every soldier is prepared to lay down his life for the mission if need be. For the other members of the unit, seeing their fellow soldier fall in line of the duty is one of the most difficult things to endure, but they endure it. They endure it because they know the person who is laying down his life needs them too. They need their sacrifice to mean something so they can protect the other members of their unit, their family, and those at home who can't protect themselves. It's tough to watch a fellow soldier lay down their life, but the best way to honor them is to finish the mission."

Tracy pulled her head away from Tobias and screamed at Mackenzie, "You don't understand! I don't feel like I am losing a family member or losing another soldier. I feel like a part of me is dying! I feel like an entire section of my mind is slipping away and there's nothing I can do about it!" She threw her hands into the air. "How am I supposed to accept that? How I am supposed to live with the fact that a part of me I only recently embraced is going to die?"

She shook her head. "Losing ROC 3 caused Sheena Green's mind to shut down. Losing ROC 1 caused Tobias to slip into depression. They're soldiers trained to deal with loss? I am a scientist, how am I supposed to deal with losing MEG 1?"

Tobias pulled Tracy close to him. "Together. We deal with it together." He looked into her eyes. "You're right. I was fighting depression after the loss of ROC 1. I felt like there was a void in my mind after I lost him. At first, I was able to fill that void with revenge by hunting down Rol-Hama and killing him. After that though, the sense of loss and the sense of companionship that I had denied ROC 1 started to get me. I was finding it difficult to face each day because I felt incomplete. I felt that way until I started to open up to you. You helped to fill that void in me. You helped me to learn to open myself up to MEG 2 by showing me what it meant to expose my thoughts, feelings, desires, and fears to someone else." He shook his head. "I know that ROC 1 died without me ever letting him in. I know he died thinking I never cared about him. I can never undo that feeling and I'll have to live with it the rest of my life."

He briefly kissed Tracy before he started talking again. "The gift you have given me by teaching how to open myself up has allowed me to open myself to MEG 2. I've shared MEG 2's mind. I know he feels wanted and accepted by me. I also know he's shared my mind. I know that my desire to complete our mission, to finish saving the world, is as important to him as it is to me." He shook his head. "I know MEG 2 is dying. I know he's aware of how scared I am of the Shojo because of his resemblance to the Sasquatch. I know all of these things and while they are all important, I know what really matters to me and MEG 2. I know above all else, MEG 2 wants to complete this mission. I know he wants us to face the Shojo. He wants us to face the Shojo so that we can complete our mission and so I can overcome my fear. MEG 2 and I are deeply connected at this point. No matter what happens to him, he wants to rid my mind of the fear I have of the Sasquatch and ROC 1's death." He hugged Tracy hard. "Most importantly, I know that I love you. No matter what happens, I will be there to help you work through whatever we face after this over together."

He pulled Tracy off his chest and looked into her eyes again. "Now ask yourself again, is MEG 1 going to die from the wounds she has suffered?"

Tracy wailed. "Yes! She's going to die."

Tobias spoke as softly as he could, "Now think about this next question. What does she want? Don't think about what you want for her. Think about what she wants, not only for herself but also for you."

Tracy shook her head. "She's doesn't want to die, but she knows she's dying." Tracy tried to continue talking, but the words wouldn't come out. She just looked at Tobias and shook her head as more tears streamed down her face.

Tobias ran his hand through her hair. "It's okay. Say it out loud. It will make you feel better."

Tracy nodded. "She wants me to be happy. She knows how much you mean to me. She knows that I love you. She wants to finish the mission and kill the Shojo so you and I can go on with our lives and be happy."

Tobias smiled. "All right then. I think if the MEGs last request is to finish the mission, that we should honor their wishes."

Tracy slowly nodded and then she looked over at Mackenzie and Jillian. "Listen to me, this is it! After the Shojo is gone, the syncing program ends. Bixby and Munroe will stay connected to the ROCs, but I can't put anyone else through this. Now that I understand the consequence of losing someone you have shared a mind with, I can't subject other people to it." She shook her head. "I can only imagine this is what it's like for a parent to lose a child. To lose someone who is their own person but at the same time a part of you." She looked over at Tobias. "My God, you've had to endure this twice now." She shook her head again. "I'm so sorry, Tobias. You've had to endure this pain because of something I helped create." She hugged him again. "Like you said, I can't undo the pain I have caused, but I can try to improve going forward. Once this is over, you and I will help each other through the healing process together." She kissed Tobias and then looked over at Mackenzie and Jillian. They were standing there silently staring at them. "We are ready now. Let's intercept the Shojo and put an end to this nightmare."

Mackenzie nodded. "If the MEGs move at top speed, they can reach the Shojo in eight hours."

Jillian sighed. "I want you two to understand what that means. Moving at top speed will tax the MEGs even more. Pushing them harder will cause both you and them physical and mental pain. It will also cut down on the twelve-hour timeframe I had suggested. Is that something the two of you can endure?"

Tracy and Tobias both nodded and then they headed over toward their neurolink recliners. Tracy hugged Tobias before climbing into her recliner. She watched him walk the ten steps from her recliner to his. Once Tobias had placed his neurolink on his head, Tracy did the same.

As the two pilots were syncing with their MEGs, Jillian looked over at Mackenzie. "We have to keep a close eye on this battle. If one of the MEGs is about to die, we will have to run over and disconnect our pilots from the shark. With the state their minds are in right now, they may not be able to disconnect themselves when the time comes."

The usual flash of light Tracy saw when entering MEG 1's mind was accompanied by agonizing pain. MEG 1 was badly injured. At a rough guess, Tracy would have surmised that nearly thirty percent of the shark's scales had been torn off her body. With each stroke of her tail, MEG 1 forced stinging salt water into her exposed muscles and tendons. Tracy first asked MEG 1 to forgive her for what she needed to do next and then she directed the cybernetic shark to swim as fast as she could toward their next target. The shark increased her speed and Tracy dug her hands into the sides of her recliner to help her deal with the influx of pain the shark was experiencing.

INDIAN OCEAN OFF THE COAST OF AUSTRALIA

The nonstop humming sound of the Sea Hunter's motor continued to further enrage the Shojo. The beast could see his newest target moving through the ocean ahead of him and he was determined to destroy it. The hairy monster surfaced behind the Sea Hunter just as he had done with the first drone. The Shojo placed his arms out in front of himself to swat away the torpedoes he expected the drone to fire at him. The intelligent monster's prediction proved correct as twin torpedoes jumped out of the back of the drone and streaked toward him. The Shojo knocked the projectiles aside and then he swam up to the drone. When he was alongside the Sea Hunter, the monster lifted his fist into the air and brought it crashing down onto the drone.

With a single blow from the powerful Shojo, the Sea Hunter was shattered into hundreds of pieces. The beast let loose a roar that echoed across the sky. He then slipped down back beneath the waves. The Shojo could feel the anger and urge to destroy slipping out of his body. He was swimming to the ocean floor to sleep when he sensed two large creatures nearby. The simian kaiju was not completely sure what the creatures were, but what he did know was that they were invading his territory. The Shojo's own territorial instincts were further inflamed by Rol-Hama's implant. The Shojo beat his chest in a show of strength and then he started swimming out to lay waste to this new challenge.

****

For the past three hours, Tracy had been doing her best to ignore the pain she was feeling from MEG 1 and the stream of blood that was trailing behind the shark as they cruised toward their final battle. Knowing that this was the last time she would ever by synced with MEG 1, Tracy focused on all of the amazing things that sharing a mind with a giant shark afforded her. As she done back in the Chesapeake Bay, Tracy took in everything that MEG 1 was sensing. Tracy made a note of every fish she could sense swimming in the water, every crustacean crawling on the ocean floor, and the scents of whales and dolphins as they swam away from the massive shark patrolling their waters. Everything that she experienced while with MEG 1 would help her to remember her friend when she was gone.

Tracy had just shifted MEG 1's eyes toward a bloom of brightly colored jellyfish when a message flashed in front of her eyes.

The Shojo has turned and is heading toward you. Be ready. For an ape who lives underwater, he can really move. His stats are as follows. Two hundred and seventy-five feet tall. He is extremely durable and physically powerful. You should confront him within the hour. Good luck. I know that you two can put an end to this nightmare.

Tracy took a deep breath and thought, *All right. girl. This is it. If this is going to be our last ride together, let's make it count. That Sasquatch-wannabe is going down today.*

Tracy could tell that MEG 1 shared her sentiments toward the Shojo. It comforted Tracy to some extent to know that she and MEG 1 were unified in their purpose as they approached the end of their time together. There was erratic movement to the left of the cybernetic shark which caused MEG 1 to shift her eyes toward it. Tracy saw MEG 2 shaking his head and swimming in an odd pattern. She briefly thought to herself, *Come on, Tobias. You can do this.*

The two MEGs swam on for another thirty minutes until a dark form began to take shape in front of them. Tracy's body shuddered with fear at the sight of the approaching Shojo. Tracy thought the strange beast resembled Chewbacca from the Star Wars franchise with its thick hairy body and long limbs. The main difference between the Wookiee and the monster was the flat, elongated face of the Shojo. Tracy watched as that face bared its fangs and roared a challenge at the approaching sharks.

Tracy prepared to have MEG 1 attack the beast when she felt more erratic movements from beside her. MEG 1 looked over and Tracy saw MEG 2 thrashing wildly in the water. She immediately knew what was happening. The stress of losing MEG 2 and the similarities between the Shojo and the Sasquatch were causing Tobias to have a post-traumatic breakdown.

Tracy shifted MEG 1's eyes forward to see the Shojo quickly closing in on the MEGs. Tracy knew she needed MEG 2 to defeat the Shojo and she took a desperate gamble. First, she directed MEG 1 to swim a holding pattern around the cryptid. Then, she pulled the neurolink helmet off her head and found herself back in Baltimore. Tracy looked over to see Tobias convulsing in his recliner.

Mackenzie yelled from behind his computer, "What are you doing? Sync back up with MEG 1 now! Crow is freaking out and we need at least one of you synced with a shark if we have any hope of killing that monster!"

Tracy jumped out of her recliner and she started trying to push it toward Tobias. She yelled at Mackenzie and Jillian, "Help me push this over toward Tobias! Bixby and Munroe are able to sync with their ROCs much better when they are in physical contact! If I can get close enough to touch him, I may be able to help Tobias get himself under control."

Jillian immediately leapt up and started helping her friend. Mackenzie ran over and yelled, "We had to reconfigure all of Bixby's and Munroe's wiring to get them next to each other! If we push the table closer to Crow, will the wires even reach that far?"

Tracy groaned as she pushed her recliner as hard as she could. "They had better stretch far enough. If they don't, the Shojo will take MEG 1 apart whether I am connected to her or not. We need both MEGs to beat that monster!"

The three friends pushed on the heavy recliner as hard as they could and it started to slide across the floor. After moving half the distance toward Tobias, the recliner stopped. Mackenzie yelled, "One more push! Go!" They pushed one more time before Jillian yelled out, "That's it." She pointed to the taut cords from Tracy's neurolink helmet to the ceiling. "If we push it any further, the cords will snap and she won't be able to reconnect with MEG 1."

Tracy climbed into her recliner and held her hand over the side. "Quick, put the neurolink helmet back on my head. Then take Tobias' hand and put it in mine."

Jillian pulled the helmet over Tracy's head and she found herself looking through MEG 1's eyes to see the Shojo right in front of her face with his fist coming down toward her. The Shojo's fist hit MEG 1 so hard that Tracy could feel the shark's skull fold inward. Had the shark's skeleton been made of bone instead of the much more pliable cartilage, she was sure MEG 1's skull would have been crushed. While it didn't kill MEG 1, the blow was still powerful enough to stun the giant shark. Tracy was urging MEG 1 to swim away from the Shojo, but the shark was unable to comply. The Shojo moved toward MEG 1 and then struck her in the jaw with such force that the shark spun a full one hundred and eighty degrees in the water.

Jillian grabbed a hold of Tobias' arm and stretched it out as far it would reach. She then placed his hand in Tracy's hand and interlocked their fingers. She then turned to Mackenzie. "Get back on the computer and tell me what's happening. I am going to stay next to them. The minute it looks like one of the MEGs is going to die, let me know and I'll disconnect them from the neurolink."

Mackenzie nodded and ran back to observe the battle.

The moment he felt Tracy's hand in his, Tobias began to calm down. Having the comfort of being reassured that Tracy was there helped Tobias to refocus his mind. His mind cleared to the point where he could see MEG 1 being battered by the Shojo. Knowing the love of his life was being pummeled to death allowed Tobias to push past his fear of the Shojo, and of losing MEG 2.

The Shojo was pulling his right arm back to strike MEG 1 again when Tobias had MEG 2 attack. MEG 2 sank his teeth into the Shojo's right tricep. The shark shook his arm violently, causing as much damage as he could to the aquatic ape's arm. The Shojo grimaced in pain as he swung his left arm around and struck MEG 2 in the face. Tobias felt several teeth fall off as the Shojo's blow forced MEG 2 off his arm.

MEG 1 was stunned from the Shojo's blow. Tracy had the shark shake her body to reorient herself but that caused the wounds from the battle with Otaka to stretch and tear. Blood spurted out from wounds that had partially healed over and MEG 1 shook her head as the pain became too much for her endure. Tracy had MEG 1 shift her eyes back to the Shojo just in time to see the simian monster punch MEG 2 off his arm.

MEG 2 was floating senselessly in front of the Shojo when the monster delivered a hammer fist to the top of the shark's head that sent him sinking toward the ocean floor.

Seeing MEG 2 and Tobias in trouble sent a surge of adrenaline coursing through Tracy's body. MEG 1 felt the surge as well and it helped the shark to reorient herself to her surroundings. Tracy saw the Shojo grab the senseless MEG 2 by his snout. The Shojo snarled at the injured shark and then delivered a punch to his stomach. The blow was so powerful that it disrupted MEG 2's breathing and caused him to vomit up the parts of Otaka he had ingested. The Shojo held his grip on MEG 2 as he brushed the carrion away from his face. He then snarled and punched MEG 2 for a second time.

Tracy could see that MEG 2 was only seconds away from dying if he didn't escape from the Shojo's grasp. She took a look at the beast and when she saw a weak point that she could exploit, Tracy had MEG 1 swim toward the Shojo's legs. When MEG 1 had almost reached the Shojo, Tracy had the shark shift to the right so that her knife-like pectoral fin sliced into the ape's hamstring.

The Shojo winced in pain, released his grip on MEG 2, and grabbed his wounded hamstring. MEG 1 brushed up against MEG 2 in an attempt to bring the stunned shark back to his senses. She then turned to see the Shojo sinking to the bottom of the ocean. When the Shojo landed on the ocean floor, Tracy could see that he was still favoring his injured leg. She hoped that MEG 1 had cut deep enough into the tendon to keep the Shojo from swimming anymore. If the Shojo was stuck on the ocean floor while the MEGs were able to swim, she thought it would give Tobias and her a much-needed advantage.

Tracy had MEG 1 take up a circling pattern around the Shojo and MEG 2 quickly joined in. MEG 1 swam toward the Shojo, forcing the monster to pay attention to her. Just before MEG 1 reached the monster, Tracy directed her to swim toward the surface. The sharp change in direction caused the wounds in MEG 1's scales to tear open even more. The maneuver was painful, but it succeeded in gaining the Shojo's attention. As the Shojo's eyes followed MEG 1, MEG 2 swam up behind him and used his pectoral fin slice into the Shojo's hip.

The Shojo swung out at MEG 2 as he swam past him and then he grabbed his injured hip. While the Shojo was turned away from MEG 1, Tracy took the chance to attack. She had MEG 1 dive toward the Shojo and use her pectoral fin to cut open a wide gap in the Shojo's back. The ape monster swung at MEG 1 as MEG 2 charged at the monster to attack him again.

MEG 2 had almost reached the Shojo when the beast suddenly turned around and grabbed the shark by his nose and lower jaw. The intelligent monster had timed MEG 2's hit and run attack and now the shark was at his mercy. Tobias had MEG 2 activate his electric charge. The shock caused the Shojo's body to glow blue as all the hair on his body stood on end. Despite the pain he was in, the Shojo refused to release his grip.

From his computer console, Mackenzie yelled, "Pull out Crow! Pull Out Crow!" Jillian yanked the neurolink helmet off Tobias' head.

When Tobias saw Jillian, he yelled, "Put me back in!"

Mackenzie called out, "It's too late. There is nothing to put you back in to."

Tracy urged MEG 1 to swim as fast as she could toward the Shojo as he held

MEG 2 in his hands. The Shojo snarled at the shark in his grasp and then tore its head in two. The Shojo was covered by a cloud of blood as he dropped the remains of MEG 2 to the ocean floor.

Tracy screamed as MEG 1 swam into the cloud of blood. The Shojo's vision was obscured by the crimson mist surrounding him. He took a step forward to move out of the cloud when she suddenly saw MEG 1's face in front of his. MEG 1's eyes rolled in the back of her head as she closed her jaws on the Shojo's head. Tracy screamed as she had MEG 1 bite into the Shojo's face over and over again. In an act of desperation, the Shojo plunged his claw into MEG 1's stomach. Tracy's body went rigid when she felt the Shojo's hand grab MEG 1's spine.

Tracy saw a flash of light and then she saw herself looking up at Tobias and Jillian. She yelled, "What happened? Is she still alive?"

Tracy stood and ran over to Mackenzie's computer. His screen was still streaming the image from MEG 1's vision. It was clear that MEG 1 was on her side lying on the bottom of the ocean. The shark rolled her eyes to the left to show see the Shojo stumbling along the bottom of the ocean. The ape's head was a bloody mess and in his claw they could see a large portion of MEG 1's spine. The Shojo took two more steps before his body slumped over and then started floating to toward the surface.

The feed from MEG 1's vision slowly went black. Mackenzie looked at Tracy. "The vitals for both MEG 1 and The Shojo have flat-lined." He placed his hand on Tracy's shoulder. "You did it. The Shojo's dead."

Tracy began to tear up. "More importantly, she's no longer in pain." Tracy walked over to Tobias and she hugged him. "They gave their lives to save all of us."

Tobias whispered to her, "I know."

EPILOGUE

For the next three days, Tracy and Tobias stayed in their quarters. The first day, the physically and emotionally exhausted couple slept for nearly twenty-four hours. When Tracy woke up on the second day, she saw Tobias making breakfast in their kitchen as the news was running on the television. The news anchor was reporting how the U.S. government had eradicated the sea monsters unleashed by Rol-Hama and that worldwide shipping had been restored. The news showed scenes of tanker trucks pulling into gas stations to refill distribution tanks. Medical trucks delivering medical supplies to hospitals. Grocery stores opening their bay doors as trucks pulled up with food to be unloaded. Scene after scene was shown accompanied by happy, cheering people. As Tracy stared at the elated masses, it only deepened the sadness she felt over the loss of MEG 1.

She walked over and sat down at the table. She looked at Tobias. "How do you deal with it? How do you deal with sharing your mind with another living creature and then just having them gone? How do you accept the fact you know what it's like to swim in the deepest part of the ocean and know you'll never do it again? When you were connected to ROC 1, you knew what it was like to fly. How did you get over losing that feeling?" On the television, the news anchor mentioned an unconfirmed report of Tobias Crow being part of the effort to exterminate the sea monster threat.

Tobias sighed when he heard his name mentioned. He then turned away from the pancakes he was making and shrugged. "I didn't get over it. It's something special I had and now it's gone forever. I am still trying to figure how to get past it. In the meantime, I am just trying to get on with my life."

He walked over and hugged Tracy. "I'm finding new ways to make connections with people and creating something else that's special to me." He kissed the top of her head. "I need to get out of here. Do you want to go for a run with me?"

Tracy looked at the door. "I'm just not ready. I can't stop thinking about what I've lost. I mean, how can I ever go for a run again without comparing it to swimming through depths of the world's oceans?" She shrugged. "Every time that I think about how MEG 1 is dead, I just feel hollow and incomplete. I'm not ready to go out there and face the world. You go for a run. I'll be fine."

Tobias hugged her. "I'm not going to leave you here by yourself feeling the way you are. We can just watch a movie or something."

Tracy pushed him away. "I'm not really in the mood for a movie. Honestly, if I think I'm holding you back from going from a run and coping with what's happened, I'll only feel worse. Please, go for a run. I'll see you when you get back."

Tobias could see how much Tracy was hurting and he didn't want to add on to her pain. He kissed her on the head. "Okay, I'll go. Just remember that I love you."

Tracy hugged him. "I know. I love you too." She then walked back over to her bed and laid back down.

Tobias took one last look at her before he walked out the door. He knew he needed to do something to help Tracy. He had an idea about something that might help her work through her grieving, but he was terrified about enacting it. Tobias remembered how Tracy had helped him get over his irrational fear of the Shojo and of losing MEG 2. He bit his lip and walked toward Mackenzie's office.

Tobias returned several hours later to find Tracy still in bed. He kissed her. "I'm back."

She nodded. "How was your run?"

Tobias nodded when he realized Tracy had no idea how long he had been gone. He smiled. "It was good. I ran into Mackenzie on the way back. He said he needs to see us for a final briefing regarding our mission. The meeting is in an hour, in the briefing room. So we need to shower and get dressed."

Tracy's eye's flared up with anger. "That man is inhuman! He knows how much the loss of the MEGs hurt us and he wants us to go talk about it!" She started to get out of bed. "I may not be ready to talk about what happened to the MEGs, but maybe it will help to go chew his ass out!" She sat up and started walking toward the shower. "In a world with a giant aquatic ape and a deformed mermaid, he's the real monster!" Tracy stood up and started walking toward the door. "The hell with an hour from now and shower. I am going to tell that man off right now!"

Tobias grabbed her arm. "He said he had a meeting with the president when I saw him. So I don't think you can get to him now anyway. You've been in bed for two days. A shower might help you feel a little better." He smiled at her. "I also know you well enough to know you'll still be mad an hour from now."

Tracy threw her hands out in disgust. "Fine. I'll shower and get dressed, but then I'm telling Mackenzie how freaking horrible he is and then I'm quitting my job here."

Tracy stormed off and jumped into the shower.

An hour later, she was storming ahead of Tobias as she made her way to the briefing room. She threw open the door to see Mackenzie, Jillian Crean, and surprisingly Bixby and Munroe sitting there. She glared at Mackenzie and then walked over to him. "You have to be the most heartless piece of scum walking the face of this Earth to call us down for debriefing now! Do you know what I am going through? Do you know how much pain I am in? How alone I feel after losing what I have lost?"

Mackenzie didn't reply; he simply sat there silently with an odd look on his face. Tracy was about to start yelling at him when a familiar tune started to play throughout the briefing room.

Tracy turned around to see Tobias nervously smiling with a microphone in his hand. He brought the mic up to his mouth and said, "Tracy, believe it or not, this may be the hardest thing I have ever done. I really need you up here to help me through this." He pointed to the large screen in the center of the room. Tracy looked at it to see the word *Female* in pink and *Male* in blue.

The words *They say we're young and we don't know. We won't find until we grow* suddenly appeared on the screen highlighted in pink.

The words changed to blue as Tobias sheepishly brought the microphone up to his mouth. "Well I don't know if all that's true, 'cause you got me and baby I got you." He walked over toward Tracy with a second microphone and he handed to Tracy, quickly saying, "We sing this next part together. Please don't leave me hanging on this."

Tracy began to smile as she took the microphone from Tobias and looked toward the screen. They both raised the microphones to their mouths and sang, "Babe, I got you babe, I got you babe."

For the first time in weeks, Tracy laughed. She and Tobias sang the rest of song off-key and with words missing. When the song was finished, everyone cheered as food and drinks were brought into the briefing room. Tobias grabbed Tracy's hand and then they bowed. They placed their microphones next to the large screen. Tracy hugged Tobias and whispered, "Thank you."

He shrugged. "You gave me the courage to face an underwater Sasquatch. The least I could do was muster that same courage to sing a song with you and remind you that even with all that you lost, there's still a lot of joy to be found in your life." He smiled. "Like I sang, you've got me and you always will."

She placed her forehead against his and smiled. "I know."

THE END

CHECK OUT OTHER GREAT DEEP SEA THRILLERS

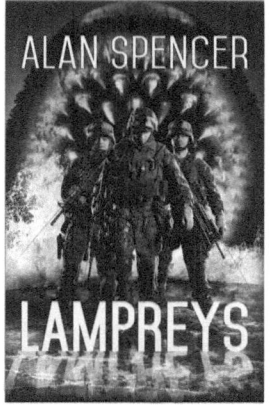

LAMPREYS
by Alan Spencer

A secret government tactical team is sent to perform a clean sweep of a private research installation. Horrible atrocities lurk within the abandoned corridors. Mutated sea creatures with insane killing abilities are waiting to suck the blood and meat from their prey.

Unemployed college professor Conrad Garfield is forced to assist and is soon separated from the team. Alone and afraid, Conrad must use his wits to battle mutated lampreys, infected scientists and go head-to-head with the biggest monstrosity of all.

Can Conrad survive, or will the deadly monsters suck the very life from his body?

DEEP DEVOTION
by M.C. Norris

Rising from the depths, a mind-bending monster unleashes a wave of terror across the American heartland. Kate Browning, a Kansas City EMT confronts her paralyzing fear of water when she traces the source of a deadly parasitic affliction to the Gulf of Mexico. Cooperating with a marine biologist, she travels to Florida in an effort to save the life of one very special patient, but the source of the epidemic happens to be the nest of a terrifying monster, one that last rose from the depths to annihilate the lost continent of Atlantis.

Leviathan, destroyer, devoted lifemate and parent, the abomination is not going to take the extermination of its brood well.

CHECK OUT OTHER GREAT
DEEP SEA THRILLERS

PREHISTORIC BEASTS AND WHERE TO FIGHT THEM
by Hugo Navikov

IN THE DEPTHS, SOMETHING WAITS ...

Acclaimed film director Jake Bentneus pilots a custom submersible to the bottom of Challenger Deep in the Pacific, the deepest point of any ocean of Earth. But something lurks at the hot hydrothermal vents, a creature—a dinosaur—too big to exist.

Gigadon.

It not only exists, but it follows him, hungrily, back to the surface. Later, a barely living Bentneus offers a $1 billion prize to anyone who can find and kill the monster. His best bet is renowned ichthyopaleontologist Sean Muir, who had predicted adapted dinosaurs lived at the bottom of the ocean.

MEGALODON: APEX PREDATOR
by S.J. Larsson

English adventurer Sir Jeffery Mallory charters a ship for a top secret expedition to Antarctica. What starts out as a search and capture mission soon turns into a terrifying fight for survival as the crew come face to face with the fiercest ocean predator to have ever existed- Carcharodon Megalodon. Alone and with no hope of rescue the crew will need all their resources if they are to survive not only a 60 foot shark but also the harsh Antarctic conditions. Megalodon: Apex Predator is a deep-sea adventure filled with action, twists and savage prehistoric sharks.

CHECK OUT OTHER GREAT DEEP SEA THRILLERS

LOCH NESS REVENGE
by Hunter Shea

Deep in the murky waters of Loch Ness, the creature known as Nessie has returned. Twins Natalie and Austin McQueen watched in horror as their parents were devoured by the world's most infamous lake monster. Two decades later, it's their turn to hunt the legend. But what lurks in the Loch is not what they expected. Nessie is devouring everything in and around the Loch, and it's not alone. Hell has come to the Scottish Highlands. In a fierce battle between man and monster, the world may never be the same. Praise for THEY RISE : "Outrageous, balls to the wall...made me yearn for 3D glasses and a tub of popcorn, extra butter!" – The Eyes of Madness "A fast-paced, gore-heavy splatter fest of sharksploitation." The Werd "A rocket paced horror story. I enjoyed the hell out of this book." Shotgun Logic Reviews

TERROR FROM THE DEEP
by Alex Laybourne

When deep sea seismic activity cracks open a world hidden for millions of years, terrifying leviathans of the deep are unleashed to rampage off the coast of Mexico. Trapped on an island resort, MMA fighter Troy Deane leads a small group of survivors in the fight of their lives against pre-historic beasts long thought extinct. The terror from the deep has awoken, and it will take everything they have to conquer it.

www.ingramcontent.com/pod-product-compliance
Lightning Source LLC
Chambersburg PA
CBHW051958170626
46808CB00007B/2686